MW01088981

Michelle the Archangel
The Return of Beth

A Fake History
By Mike Joyner
Copyright ©2019

ISBN: 9781099994241
Imprint: Independently published

To Teri, who has taught me that no one cares how much you know until they know how much you care.

Introduction & Forward by Cole Stephensen

Michelle the Archangel by Michael J. (Mike) Joyner will emerge as an instant classic in the emerging scholarly and literary genre known as Pop History. Dr. Joyner is one of the leading freelance practitioners of Pop History, and his book is a behind-the-scenes account of Michelle Pailer and how she became the first female president of the United States. It also covers some of what happened following that event along with key insights about the presidential elections of 2020, 2024, and 2028. Much of what is written is generally known, but this book reports new behind-the-scenes details about the events surrounding Pailer's ascension to the presidency. It also paints vivid portraits of both the well- and lesser-known players involved. Of caution, *Michelle the Archangel* is not written with a linear timeline and weaves back and forth between the present, recent past, and more distant past. This is required to add context to the complex factors that have shaped, and continue to shape, the events that have happened more recently. There is also a tendency to engage in "armchair psychology" about former President Schrimpf and some of his followers. Dr. Joyner has avoided this temptation and focuses on the facts. Pop History has been criticized by the academy and the *New Yorker* demographic as superficial, incoherent, and even "fake history." However, given the attention span and reading habits of modern audiences, the Pop History approach is effective because it serves as a combination historical Rorschach test and linked conceptual haikus that allow the discerning reader to filter, deconstruct, and even dig deeper into the textual material. The reader is of course also free to simply read the book uncritically and take it at face value. As always with Pop History, some of what is on the written page has sort of happened, some has almost happened, and some might still happen.

Cole Stephenson, Ph.D. is the UBS/Beale Professor of Pop History at the University of Southern California. He is a former member of the American Academy of Arts and Sciences.

1. How the Democrats Lost in 2020: A Synopsis

Entering the 2020 election, President Richard Schrimpf's poll numbers were in the toilet. The economy was strong, but via social media and an obsessive focus on feeding into the anxieties of his base, Schrimpf had managed to alienate all but his most hard-core supporters. There was a steady stream of new scandals including the hiring of undocumented "dancers" at the Schrimpf Organization's gentlemen's (strip) clubs now managed by his son Richie. People also started to note that his social media bark was louder than his legislative bite and that he mostly backed off or didn't have the discipline or attention span or political clout to make his many "policy ideas" stick. One day the border with Mexico was going to close, the next day some EPIC deal was signed. The same for China, NATO, and the Middle East. The only consistent messages were that President Schrimpf was the center of the universe and that North Korea and Russia were being run by some "fine people."

His prospects of reelection started to look even worse when the neofascist political commentator Buck Patrick entered the New Hampshire Republican primary and offered to debate Schrimpf at the "strip club of his choice." However, in August the Democrats gave Schrimpf a political gift. On the first multiballot convention since the 1950s, they nominated Representative Sandy Bernard of Berkeley, California, on the 15th ballot. Bernard was the first transgender person elected to the U.S. Congress after serving as mayor of Berkeley, California. While she was a moderate for a Democrat, the attack ads and social media work from "unaffiliated" groups started right away. The most effective ones centered on a discussion of "gender reassignment surgery on demand." The fringe-of-the-fringe went even further and accused the Bernard campaign of seeking "mandatory gender reassignment."

Even more damaging to her candidacy was the fact that as mayor of Berkeley she had championed a fast food tax that was highly effective in reducing obesity in the schools and increasing funding for social services.
President Schrimpf was remarkably silent on the transgender topic but spoke out forcefully in favor of fast food. He let Vice President Michelle Pailer rally the social conservatives on the transgender issues while appearing reasonable in front of the mainstream media—he focused on "Keeping America Safe for Big Macs." Pailer's focus on

social issues breathed new life into her career and was a welcome respite from going to state funerals, endless goodwill trips to obscure countries, and generally trying to clean up the various unforced political errors that the President routinely made. She figured that after Schrimpf lost, her speaking career would skyrocket with fees in excess of $50,000 per speech plus book deals to go with a return gig on Fox News.

Unfortunately for Vice President Pailer, Schrimpf (as he had in 2016) won by the narrowest of margins in the Electoral College while again losing the popular vote. This set off a debate among the pollsters, political scientists, and commentators about why this happened. The early consensus was that the country was ready for a transgender president but not fast food taxes. The experts at the FiveThirtyEight prognostication and analytics website ran millions of simulations showing that Bernard had a 97% chance of winning if fast food had not been an issue in the election.

2. 2016: The Road to the Vice Presidency

Michelle Pailer's term as governor of Minnesota ended after the 2014 (she was elected in 2010) gubernatorial election. She did not seek reelection. Her polling numbers were not good, her husband had health issues, the pay was marginal, and there were lucrative opportunities on the speaking circuit that she could leverage as an emerging icon of the Religious Right. This was a shrewd career move, and she was a natural on the commentary and speaking circuits. Nine months after leaving office, Fox News signed her for big money and set up a small studio in her home so she could work remotely.

As the 2016 primaries progressed, Richard Schrimpf connected with forgotten voters in the so-called "wrestling dad" voter demographic like no other candidate in history. Schrimpf's background was in business, and he had leveraged his family's long history in the arcade and carnival industry in the northeastern U.S. to develop novel products sold via direct-to-consumer TV marketing. His most notable success started in the late 1970s when he bought the struggling "National Hair Institute" brand and turned it into the most successful telemarketing venture ever. He had considered renaming NHI the "International" or even "Intergalactic" Hair Institute, but the marketing people told him it was important to send a "consistent" message that the Institute's products were for "red-blooded American men." They also vetoed "Intergalactic," telling Schrimpf the brand might get confused with things going on in the UFO and alien abduction subculture. Schrimpf reluctantly agreed with his advisors but only after asking, "What about the cover-up at Area 51?"

A shrewd promoter, in the early 1980s he next bought the rights to the failing International Wrestling Alliance (IWA), and it ultimately became the most popular and most watched professional wrestling circuit with a global reach. It was, in his words, "huge" and served as a platform for the Schrimpf family to engage in a wide array of co-branding activities. These included a string of IWA Gold "gentlemen's clubs," and Schrimpf was the first person to see the business opportunities for Western-style professional wrestling in Russia and China.

In the late 1990s, the Schrimpf organization started buying distressed golf properties up and down the East Coast with the backing of a syndicate of investors from Russia and China. The plan, which has been hugely successful, was to bring a "high-class" version of the Hooter's business model to the golf course and country club industry. All beverage cart drivers at Schrimpf clubs were big-breasted young women with at least D cups. As the members' preferences in women changed over the years, a major challenge in the 2000s was finding Asian women who were big enough. This led his eldest son Richie to negotiate volume discounts and a lucrative incentive plan with one of the top plastic surgeons in Miami. This initiative ultimately evolved into a breast augmentation center franchising venture—Chesty's—that was co-branded with the hair products, IWA, and golf course chain.

That Schrimpf had been married four times and fathered six children was no major impediment to his candidacy. Nor was the fact that his fourth wife Tatiana, who was born in 1978, was originally from St. Petersburg, Russia, where she obtained a graduate degree in jewelry design from the former State Institute of Mineralogy.

Using skills he had honed in the private sector, Schrimpf turned debate after debate and each public appearance into the political equivalent of his WrestleMaxia brand full of Masked Mexican Bandito Villains and a cast of other bad guys and threats. The cable channels were transfixed, and he received billions of dollars of free TV time. When the *New York Times, Washington Post*, and CNN called him out on his fantasy-based statements, he went after the "pointy headed elites" who secretly wanted to let hordes of "bad hombres" cross the southern border "at will" to rob your house, sell drugs to your kids, and rape your daughters.

His Republican foes had no idea how to respond when the Schrimpf circus came to town and all died political deaths from an apparently contagious form of flat feet.

After securing the nomination, Schrimpf—who was notoriously immune from advice of any sort—took some when told that as a four-times-married owner of essentially high-end strip clubs, he needed to secure the support of the Evangelical Christian Right to avoid a blowout. His only response was, "Who has the best numbers?" The pollsters said it was an easy call and that Michelle Pailer was by far and away the most dynamic political figure among "values voters." When he had been interviewed by her on TV, his only thought was that 25 years ago the statuesque and blonde Pailer must have been as good-looking as his second wife. And, he could not help but think that it was too bad he did not date her "back in the day." As he saw more and more of her on Fox News, he occasionally got past her more visible assets and commented to one aid, "She is the best-looking almost 50-year-old woman I have ever seen" and added, "That girl can really sell." Nominating Pailer would also show he was not sexist and took women "seriously."

So Schrimpf was nominated and offered Pailer the slot as his running mate. Pailer and her husband Marco prayed over the offer and consulted with their pastor and other leading religious conservatives. They struggled until Robertson (Pastor Bob) Gerald, president of Archangel University, reminded them that King David and a number of other Old Testament characters were hardly models of family values and that maybe Schrimpf's nomination was a sort of 2.0 Old Testament signal "to save God's chosen people"—religious and politically conservative Americans. He posted a short essay with this justification on his widely read "Prosperity Through Prayer" website and urged his followers to reach out to her at MPailer@michellepailer.org and encourage her to join Schrimpf in his latter-day "crusade to save America."

Pastor Bob's explanation, and the emails from his followers, resonated with the Pailers, and they (the husband and wife team with Marco as the captain) accepted the nomination. When the Schrimpf and Pailer families were on the convention podium with hands raised, no one noticed as Schrimpf gave his running mate a nice squeeze on her firm and shapely ass. Pailer was not offended and actually found it sort of exciting. After all, Schrimpf was a powerful man, and she had never felt any real lust from her husband in their many years of marriage.

We will get to the full story on the lust topic a bit later in this narrative.

3. Decision 2016

The 2016 campaign against the extremely qualified Democratic nominee Beth Campbell McClintock was a nasty and uphill fight. Bethany (Beth) Joan Campbell McClintock was a trailblazer and the first woman nominated for the presidency by either major party. She had been First Lady of the United States from 1993-2001 during the presidency of her husband, Willie McClintock of Tennessee. She was later elected to the Senate and then served as Secretary of Defense in the Obama Administration. She had been active in Democratic politics since attending Smith College and the Yale Law School in the late 1960s and early 1970s.

In retrospect, the McClintock campaign underperformed due to a combination of overconfidence, social media carpet-bombing from the Russian intelligence services (the Russians were terrified of McClintock based on her service as Secretary of Defense), and the fact that the "sell by date" on the McClintock brand had come and gone. These factors, plus an aloof personal style and a tendency to spend a lot of time talking about policy minutiae, were seen as some of the elements that led to the Schrimpf/Pailer victory. The FBI director also refused to clear her of allegations that she had sent text messages "relevant to her job as Secretary of Defense" on a "nonsecure" handheld device.

Schrimpf also taunted McClintock relentlessly on every imaginable issue. His own history of boorish, if not criminal, behavior with women was countered by dredging up of an impressive collection of peccadillos that her husband, former President Willie McClintock, had been involved in. Pailer, for her part, was relentless with the evangelical crowd, who loved it when she wore her "Archangel College Swordsman" swag to campaign events. At the end of her rallies, it was not unusual for the crowd to break into the spontaneous singing of *Onward Christian Soldiers.*

In the end, the pollsters, political scientists, and commentators all felt it was the professional wrestling fans who came out in droves to vote that secured the victory for Schrimpf. In the aftermath of McClintock's defeat, President Barack Obama is rumored to have asked Vice President Joe Biden, "Joe, how the hell did Beth lose?" Biden apparently responded, "Mr. President, because she couldn't sell beer on a troopship." Obama then reportedly noted, "True enough, but she could sure make Putin's palms sweat."

4. 1968-1984: The Transformation of Michelle Jensen

Michelle Pailer was born Michelle Anita Jensen on March 25, 1968, in St. Paul, Minnesota, to Bruce and Kaye (nee Heinonen) Jensen. In the late 1950s, her dad was one of the last three-sport stars at the University of Minnesota—football, hockey, and baseball—and after a stint in the Army and some minor league baseball, he returned to the university where he was a coach and athletic administrator for many years. His wife Kaye was also a talented all-around athlete who starting at a young age had been an excellent tennis player and golfer. Her formal athletic career ended young because there were no college sports for women during her time. Kaye also attended the University of Minnesota where she met Bruce. She majored in physical education and had plans to be a teacher, but one fall night in early 1961, in the back of the Chevy Bruce had purchased with his baseball signing bonus, things went a little too far. They were married in early 1962, and four months later their first child, Steve, was born "a few months early" in the spring of 1962. Another son, Dave, followed a few years later and then Michelle in 1968.

Michelle, like her parents and older brothers, was bright, a gifted athlete, and a hard worker. She was an easy child except that she had more energy than the rest of her highly energetic family combined. She enjoyed school and attending Redeemer Lutheran Church. In the mid-1970s, her parents started jogging to stay in shape and eventually started running 10K races. She started running with them and could keep up without a problem. Eventually they let her enter the races and she started running fast. By the early 1980s, girls' cross country and track programs were well established, and as a 7th grader she started to do very well in high school races. The high school rules in Minnesota allow 7th and 8th graders to participate on high school teams. This helps small rural schools field teams. Michelle's running success continued into her freshman year when she was nationally ranked in the mile after winning the state cross country meet as a 14-year-old in 1982. College coaches were already talking to her informally, and her track times were within striking distance of the 1984 Olympic Trials.

Then something happened. Michelle finally got her period, she started getting curves, and she could not run any faster. Eventually she started running slower. She increased her training and that led to a stress fracture and a six-week layoff that added 15 more pounds of curves. In three months, Michelle had gone from a 5'-8", 115-pound girl with a heart and set of lungs on the top of some fast legs to a 5'-9," 140-pound woman who looked like a younger version of Anita Ekberg. Her running was never the same, and the constant head turning by boys and men made her skin crawl. Her brother's college friends started chatting her up. She remained a straight A student.

Michelle started to wonder if Redeemer Lutheran was right for her. She was tired of the relentless organ music, and if she had to sing *A Mighty Fortress Is Our God* one more time she thought she might throw up. All that changed when Anita Gerald (they shared a name and wasn't that cool?) invited her to Bible Study at the new Archangel Christian Church in an old warehouse in St. Paul. The church had been founded by Anita's dad Robertson (Pastor Bob) who had moved the family up from Virginia because in a dream, the Archangel Michael had come to him and directed him to the Upper Midwest "to bring a truly Protestant approach to the nominally faithful Lutherans in Minnesota." Lutherans, he thought, needed to get serious about the Gospel or risk the fire of eternal damnation. The social tolerance and political liberalism also needed to go, while guitar-backed Sunday services with modern music were needed ASAP. Another consideration was that his wife Faith was from Tower, Minnesota, and anxious to get closer to home.

This all worried Michelle's parents, but if this was teenage rebellion it sure beat sex, drugs, and alcohol. Plus Michelle continued to run and do about as well as could be expected for a girl (woman) her size. The other good thing from her Jensen's perspective—they were not blind—was that Archangel Christian Church was an early adopter of chastity training for young people. They hoped the chastity message might help keep Michelle out of the back seat of any Chevys until at least college. Kaye knew that at some point they would need to talk about sex, but why push it and why give Michelle any ideas?

5. 1984-1986: Archangel College

Pastor Bob was a visionary charismatic preacher who also had the gift of organization. Through God's grace, Archangel Christian grew faster than even he had hoped and prayed. Donations took off, and some extremely well-heeled families joined the church. At about the same time, River Crossing College, a small nondenominational and liberal "Christian" school focused on the gospel of social justice and about a mile away from Archangel Christian, went bankrupt. River Crossing was founded in 1866 and included a residential school for ambitious former slaves and their descendants. It had been a thriving place through the 1960s and early 1970s, but the message no longer resonated, enrollment was down, fundraising lagged, and both the facility and the faculty were aging.

Mack Harvey, a real estate developer who was one of the well-heeled members of Archangel Christian and on the church council, figured the whole campus could be bought at fire sale prices and used to expand Archangel Christian. Pastor Bob was intrigued, and again the Archangel Michael appeared to him in a dream and directed him to both buy the property and establish a *truly* Christian college on the grounds. When Pastor Bob shared this with Mr. Harvey, he responded that coming up with the funds would be "no problem," and he could write a check "on Monday" if needed. Mr. Harvey also suggested that some of the wooded area in the nature preserve at River Crossing (with views coincidently overlooking the Mississippi River) might be ideal for a high-end housing development. If done right, he said, "the college could ultimately pay for itself."

Pastor Bob's prayers were answered.

The next steps were straightforward. Pastor Bob was president of the renamed Archangel College. He hired experienced administrators from places like Oral Roberts University, and the first class at Archangel enrolled in the fall of 1984. It was a strictly undergraduate institution, but a couple of years later the trustees became concerned about the need for Christian-based counseling and the liberal courts. At their urging, a graduate program in psychology and a law school were started, and Mr. Harvey once again stepped into the financial breach and raised the money with "no problem."

The Archangel College logo was a sword, as in the sword of the Archangel, and its mascot was the Swordsman (the men's teams were known as "the Swordsmen," and the women's teams were known as "the Scabbards").

When Pastor Bob had one of the arts volunteers in the congregation draw up some examples of possible logos, one prototype looked a lot like a Jedi Knight with a lightsaber. He loved it, figuring it would send a hip message to the younger generation and help recruitment to the congregation. Years later, there was a spike in sales of Swordsman hoodies due to the notoriety of the Swordsmen biker gang in Southern California. That got the attention of Disney executives, who also learned about the socially conservative views championed at Archangel University (the college grew and became a university in the 2000s). Disney sued for copyright infringement, and that led to a publicity bonanza for Archangel and tripled giving to the Archangel Apostles fund. By 2010, the endowment was nearly $1 billion. In the wake of the Disney incident, some of the letters that came with the checks included comments about how Jews controlled the worldwide media and were working to undermine Christian Civilization. Pastor Bob was a big supporter of Israel, but with a bit of prayer he was able to look the other way, "no problem."

As the Archangel endowment grew, his most effective fundraising line was that "Harvard and Yale started as Christian schools whose mission was to train ministers. Since they won't, I guess we have to." That line always generated a laugh, some amens, and plenty of checks.

By the early 2000s, Pastor Bob's prayers had been even more fully answered, and the visions in his Archangel dreams continued to come true. When the former Michelle Jensen, now Michelle Pailer, was elected governor of Minnesota in 2010, he found himself reflecting on his blessings. He had no way of knowing that his biggest, most important, and most prophetic dream was years away.

6. Michelle Chooses Archangel

In 1986, she graduated number one in her high school class and scored an impressive 1500 on the SAT. By watching what she ate and training relentlessly, she kept her weight in the low 130s and was able to place in the top 10 in the Minnesota girls' cross country state meet. All of the Big 10 schools wanted her, and there was even talk of the Ivy League or a scholarship to Stanford. Her parents were hoping she might ultimately follow her older brothers to medical school.

All of this was great, but Michelle wanted to go to Archangel College. For the past two summers, she worked at the Archangel Vacation Bible School and attended Camp Swordsman located on a lake in northern Wisconsin. She loved everything about Archangel College, and her best friend Anita was going there. Tuition was modest, there were plenty of work-study opportunities and generous scholarships, the application process was simple, and she knew she could be admitted right away. Archangel had only a few sports for girls, but cross country and track were two of them and competing at the small college level would be less stressful for Michelle. Plus, she connected with Coach Blair Hayden who had been a great runner. The strict rules about not being alone with boys and the extensive chaperoning of all mixed-sex activities also appealed to her because the focus would be on academics and not socializing. There was even talk of an Archangel Law School in the works, and even though she was good at science and math, she thought she might want to be a lawyer and not a doctor like her brothers.

In short, she could not imagine any other choice.

Her parents were again concerned, but what could they do? Pastor Bob was thrilled. She and Anita would be roommates in the dorm.

7. 1986-1988: Meet Marco Pailer

Marco Pailer was an upstanding Christian young man in his middle 20s. He was a graduate student working on his master's in Christian counseling in the Psychology Department at Archangel College, and he was a teaching assistant for the undergraduate courses. In addition, he was a part-time youth pastor at Archangel Christian Church, and his Christian rock band—The Sinners—was one of the most popular in the Upper Midwest. He played lead guitar and handled most of the vocals.

His work at Archangel College easily covered his living expenses. The gigs he did with The Sinners along with cassette tape sales allowed him to live alone in a nice apartment near campus and drive a newer car. He was also able to save plenty of money and not worry when he wanted to order a pizza or eat dinner at one of the new higher-end chain restaurants that were popping up in strip malls around the Twin Cities. He could also afford to fly a couple of times a year to see his parents in Pasadena, California.

Marco was also extremely well groomed, with long sandy blonde hair. He was both handsome and pretty at the same time. His Prince Valiant hairstyle was a little dated but a perfect look for the band. Because he was from California, the guys in the band and his friends nicknamed him "Surfer." He was also buff (in the 1980s sense of the word) and spent a lot of time doing push-ups, sit-ups, and other muscle-building exercises. He was a regular at the weight room in the Archangel College Gym. Marco had a hard time putting on weight in spite of the protein powder shakes he drank daily, so he avoided jogging and focused on weight training.

His ultimate goal was to look like the classic bodybuilders he saw in his extensive collection of 1950s physical culture magazines (more 1950s Steve Reeves than 1970s Arnold Schwarzenegger). A sin of vanity for sure, but with hard work and dedication, over time his shoulders got broad, his arms and chest got bigger, and the constant use of the leg press machine cured him of bird legs. His waist was 31 inches, he was 6'-1," and he weighed 175 pounds immediately after drinking a protein shake. His chest measured 44 inches.

Marco's life was on track, and he could see himself ending up in a position like Pastor Bob's, or perhaps going full-time into Christian music, or down the road he could maybe even use the master's degree in psychology he was getting to write Christian-oriented self-help books. However, to really make it big in any of those worlds he needed a wife and family, but Marco had yet to meet the right girl, and he was too busy with his band, school, and fitness routine to date. At least this is what he told the people in the Archangel community when they asked about his social life or tried to introduce him to wholesome and attractive Christian young women.

The real issue was that Marco was just not that interested in girls. The most "physically exciting" thing he did was browse through his extensive collection of 1950s physical culture magazines. The black-and-white pictures were so artistic, the men proportioned like Greek statues, and the body-oiled look so stimulating that he retreated to the shower and touched himself. He always felt really guilty about this and didn't really understand it. To atone for his transgressions, he did 500 sit-ups within 24 hours of a shower incident. If it happened more than once per week, he did 1000 for each additional transgression. Marco was not the biggest or strongest person who frequented the Archangel weight room, but his abs were the best by far.

One day when he was at the used book and magazine store in downtown Minneapolis that stocked the vintage physical culture magazines, he browsed through some 1950s pin-up magazines that featured extremely busty women. He bought several and took them back to the apartment. For the next two weeks, every time he had the urge to leaf through the physical culture magazines, he substituted one of the pin-up magazines. Except for one with a woman tied up in a chair and a second topless woman standing over her with a riding crop, they did nothing for him. He wasn't sure, but when he looked in the mirror and flexed his abs, he wondered if they were as ripped as they were before he started what he called in his weight-training diary "the pin-up experiment." Were a couple of weeks without any extra sit-ups maybe showing?

8. Make Marco's Urges Go Away

As part of his psychology course work, Marco learned about behavioral feedback and conditioning techniques. However, the library at Archangel was not extensive, so from time to time he would go to the library at the University of Minnesota and get more in-depth information. Sometimes he even sat in on classes. It was a big place with big classes, and except for the haircut, he blended right in. At the U he learned about all sorts of things, and he became fascinated with experiments that used a combination of positive and negative feedback, frequently with electrical stimulators, to modify the behavior of animals ranging from sea slugs to birds and even chimps. If done correctly, a given stimulus could generate a response that was almost automatic. In one class they actually showed clips from the movie *A Clockwork Orange* about how criminal behavior might be changed by application of these principles to delinquent young adult males.

Marco was fascinated. Marco had an idea. Could he condition himself to respond to the pin-ups and stop responding to the 1950s bodybuilders? How could he make this happen? He next read up on electrical stimulators. Most were bulky boxes and not available on the consumer market. However, there were smaller battery-operated stimulators called TENS units (transcutaneous electrical nerve stimulation) used in physical therapy for the treatment of pain. He obtained an advanced unit and his self-experiment began.

First, Marco went to the used book store and magazine shop and carefully browsed through the vintage physical culture and pin-up magazines. He then purchased a number that were especially stimulating or, in the case of women, he thought should be especially stimulating. When he got to his apartment he carefully made an equal number of flash cards of body builders and pin-ups. Next, he used his basic knowledge of electronics, from guitar amplifiers and microphones, and modified the TENS unit so that via a toggle switch he could rapidly change the stimulation parameters. He then placed the electrodes on his forearm and experimented with the settings. Over time he was able to find settings that felt really good and ones that were painful (but not that painful) and did not cause burns or major skin irritation. He tried the same strategy on his privates, and after a few adjustments he could flip the toggle switch from A to B and go from a really pleasant sensation to one that did not feel so good and made him mildly nauseous.

9. *The Program*

Marco knew from his experiences in the weight room that the fundamental factors for success with any training program were dedication, consistency, a positive mental attitude, and the progressive overload principle. Using these fundamentals, he began using the stimulator while rapidly working his way through his deck of bodybuilder/pin-up flash cards. First he would shuffle the cards (he had about 100) so that the visual stimuli were random. Next he would attach the stimulator, adjust the settings, and make sure the toggle switch was working. He then flipped through the cards and applied the painful stimulating current when he saw a man and the pleasant current when a woman came up. At first he did this as fast as he could. As his early experiments with The Program (that was the code word he used in his weight-training diary) progressed, he extended the time he looked at each picture, and every month or so he visited the used magazine and book store and increased his collection of flash cards.

As part of the progressive overload principle, on Mondays, Wednesdays, and Fridays he did one short session of about 15 minutes with minimal settings on the stimulator. On Tuesdays, Thursdays, and Saturdays he did two-a-days with each session lasting a minimum of 30 minutes and employing maximal tolerable stimulation parameters. On Sundays he rested.

The results were slow, but after about two months the full sensation that he felt in his groin when leafing through a random physical culture magazine came on much slower. It was also less intense and generated fewer trips to the shower. By contrast, he started to like the pin-ups a bit more. If he looked at one of the magazines with a lot of riding crop photos, he even needed to make trips to the shower sometimes. After about 6 months, the success ratio was 60/40 in favor of the riding crop flash cards. He was confident that with continued hard work and dedication he could achieve a ratio of 80/20 in no time. When he got to 80/20, he thought he might switch from men vs. riding crop to riding crop vs. big breasts. Marco also speculated to himself that perhaps some sort of split pattern like advanced bodybuilders use when they work their arms three days per week and their legs the other three days per week would be even more effective in generating the psychological adaptations he sought.

The Program was working and he was thrilled, but his sit-up volume at home was declining so he had to do more ab work during his formal training sessions at the Archangel Gym. That was a minor blessing in disguise because the gym had a state-of-the-art incline board for ab work that made his six-pack harder and more defined than ever. Marco also began to wonder if there were other people with his problem, and if The Program might work for them.

10. Michelle Meets Marco

Michelle and Marco had seen each other on campus, and when the track team spent time in the weight room they were vaguely aware of each other. The weight room dress code (covered shoulders, no tights, and the early version of the compression sports bra Michelle wore) meant that not a lot of skin was exposed and that a well-built girl like Michelle would not distract the boys from their weight training. However, Marco occasionally lifted his shirt discretely to check his abs in the mirror while working out, and a couple of times Michelle caught a glimpse of them. She also saw him rip off sets of more than 20 wide-grip pull-ups followed by more than 20 bar-dips over and over. His V-shape was hard to ignore, and his hair was so beautiful. When she was not careful, thoughts of running her hands through his hair popped into her normally vigilant mind. During her sophomore year, Marco was the teaching assistant in her psych class, and she had more and more trouble suppressing such thoughts. She even caught herself wondering if he wore tight-fitting shirts on purpose to distract her.

More and more often she found herself thinking about him, especially when she was showering. Sometimes she even touched herself. She always felt guilty about this and didn't really understand it, but she did do 500 sit-ups within 24 hours of a transgression in the shower. If it happened more than once per week, she did 1,000 for each additional incident. This had the additional benefit of keeping her as lean as possible, and as a result Michelle was running almost as fast as she did when she was 14. That fall she made small college All-American in cross country.

Pastor Bob was impressed by Marco and continued to hear good things about him from both the Archangel College faculty and from parents at Archangel Church. One day in the late fall of 1987, Pastor Bob summoned Marco to his office and asked if he wanted to play a bigger role at Camp Swordsman in the summer of 1988. Marco said he would be thrilled to but was worried about some of the gigs The Sinners had already secured for the upcoming summer. He explained the potential scheduling problems to Pastor Bob, who said (with what was left of his soft Virginia accent), "Son, music may be the future of your ministry, and I am sure we can be flexible so you and the band can keep your commitments this summer." So, in addition to the stipend he would receive as assistant camp director, his income from the band would continue.

A few days later, Pastor Bob bumped into Michelle and his daughter Anita walking across campus. He was again struck by how wholesome and attractive Michelle was and immediately thought about how he might connect her with Marco.   When Michelle stopped by the parsonage one day, he asked her to run the junior high girls' cabins at Camp Swordsman that summer. The boys' and girls' cabins were on opposite sides of a small lake to prevent unauthorized contact between the sexes. Historically, the junior high campers were at high risk for fraternization, and he was confident that Michelle, an alumnus of the camp, would be vigilant and keep a lid on things.

At dinner a few days later, he told his wife what he had done. Faith approved, and because she was at camp most of the summer, she agreed to make sure Marco and Michelle spent plenty of time (supervised by her) together.

11. Camp Swordsman

Other than the zeal of its mission, there was nothing unusual about Camp Swordsman. It was one of the many summer camps located on lakes in northern Wisconsin. These camps catered to kids (and parents) from Chicago, Milwaukee, and the Twin Cities with all sorts of needs and interests.

When Marco Pailer arrived at Camp Swordsman in late May of 1988, he noted it to be in good shape except for the lack of a weight room or any strength-training equipment. He immediately set to work with the camp handyman and built a beautiful wooden pull-up, bar-dip, and incline sit-up apparatus near the lake that he could use to maintain his physique in the absence of any free weights. Marco also worked closely with Faith Gerald and members of his staff of teenaged and early 20s counselors (including Michelle) to review the curriculum for the summer. It included all sorts of fun activities plus plenty of Bible lessons and singing. Michelle for her part found the trails in and around camp an ideal training environment as she logged mile after mile in preparation for the upcoming cross country season.

The summer went off without a hitch. The campers had fun, and boy/girl fraternization by the junior high kids was kept to a minimum.

Faith was very pleased to see Marco and Michelle spending a lot of time together and noted that they were frequently taking long walks after dinner. She was also pleased that nothing physically suspicious or worrisome appeared to be happening. Faith also felt that the interest Marco was taking in and mentorship he was clearly providing to young Baker Jimerson, the camp music director and talented organ major from St. Olaf College, was a "real positive."

Pastor Bob visited Camp Swordsman from time to time and checked with Faith on what he called "Marco-Michelle progress." He was pleased to hear they were spending time together but mystified that apparently, as he put it to Faith one night in the camp director's cabin, "nothing physical" had happened. Frankly, he thought to himself in a moment of weakness, how could an obviously virile young man like Marco go all summer and not at least get Michelle to take her shirt off?

Marco must have deep faith, he thought, deeper than he had during the summer of 1967. That summer in somewhat similar circumstances, he could not control his urges and went too far with Faith one night—way too far.

No one mentioned it when Anita was born three months early.

12. 1988-1993: Dean Moon

By the late 1980s, Judge Art Moon was bored. He was one of the youngest men on the federal bench, the pay was marginal, the cases were boring, and making the Supreme Court any time soon was a long shot. The work he had done at the Department of Justice (DOJ) early in the Reagan Administration had been a lot more interesting. In early 1988 at a meeting of the Originalist Society, he heard that Archangel College was planning to open a law school whose mission was to train a new generation of conservative lawyers. The law school had been endowed by an anonymous and very generous donor, and Archangel was searching for a founding dean.

Judge Moon let it be known through the conservative legal grapevine that he would be highly interested in "learning more." His pedigree was good and his biography was compelling. He had been born in Broiler, Texas, to Emory and Jane Moon. His father was a legendary high school football coach and part-time Pentecostal lay preacher. Emory Moon was also widely credited with both inventing the wishbone offensive formation and playing a key role in the integration of high school football in Texas.

Art Moon was too small for football and served as a football manager when he attended Briles Baptist University. He rose to the rank of head manager for the 1971 season that saw Briles win the Cotton Bowl. After graduating first in his class at Briles, he matriculated at the Harvard Law School where he was the first conservative student in memory to lead the *Harvard Law Review.*

The recruitment of Judge Moon as founding dean went quickly. Archangel President (Pastor Bob) Gerald and Judge Moon found their philosophies and views of the world "convergent." Moon was hired as founding dean of the Archangel College of Law and was on the Archangel campus full-time by the fall of 1988. The first class of the school would enroll for the fall semester of 1990.

When news of the new law school became public, once again with the encouragement of Anita and Pastor Bob, Michelle Jensen once again chose Archangel. The idea of being in the first class of the new school appealed to her, and even though physical progress had been slow, she would be close to Marco. Once again her parents, Bruce and Kaye, scratched their heads and again wondered why Michelle, who had aced the LSATs and made small college All-American as a runner, didn't pick an Ivy League or Big 10 law school. She would have been a shoo-in.

13. These People

In the early 1990s, Pastor Bob began to see the "Homosexual Agenda" as a real threat to what he was building across the Archangel community in specific and his vision of a Christian America anointed by God in general. His sermons on this theme were some of his best, and the whole topic breathed new life into his ministry. He noted repeatedly that there was nothing in the Bible about "Adam and Steve."

As the sermons progressed, they resonated with Marco and he redoubled his efforts with The Program. By then he had finished his Ed.D. in counseling and psychology at North Metro State and was working with Pastor Bob to generate a line of counseling services at Archangel that focused on Christian psychology. The goal was to help members of the ever-expanding Archangel congregation deal with problems like straying teenagers, problem drinking, and adultery.

During their planning meetings, Marco said he had been paying close attention to the sermons on the challenges of the Homosexual Agenda in America and had an idea. He explained what he had learned in graduate school about operant conditioning and shared that he had been using a program based on operant conditioning to control his urges.

Marco did not go into the details of the program, and Pastor Bob assumed the urges Marco was referring to were natural urges. Urges related to what was under the tight-fitting sweaters girls like Michelle Jensen sometimes wore. The Pastor was a happily married man, but he was not blind. Maybe, he thought, The Program explained Marco's impressive self-control around Michelle when they were at Camp Swordsman several summers ago.

Pastor Bob then asked Marco a series of questions about the possibility of using a similar strategy to help men with unnatural urges. Marco said he thought it was possible, especially if the program targeted teenagers and young men "before any unnatural urges became hard-wired into their central nervous systems."

Pastor Bob commented it was his duty as a compassionate Christian to help "these people" with a scientifically based program that in conjunction with prayer, and the grace of God, might normalize their urges.

Marco had the green light to use The Program as part of the growing menu of counseling services offered at Archangel Christian Church. Demand for "urge normalization therapy," as he branded The Program, eventually became so high that The Program ultimately was spun out of Archangel and housed in the affiliated National Center for Gender Confusion.

14. 1993: Dr. and Mrs. Pailer

Marco Pailer and Michelle Jensen were married during the early summer of 1993 after her law school graduation. It was a big wedding with Pastor Bob officiating, while Bruce and Kaye Jensen wondered again what had happened to Michelle and what they had done wrong. The highlight of the ceremony was young Baker Jimerson's outstanding selection of organ music. Organ music is a major element of services at Lutheran churches, and Bruce thought to himself, "It is too bad that kid is not one of us."

The vows were very traditional with Michelle agreeing to obey Marco. The obey clause had been a sticking point for some young couples during premarital counseling with Pastor Bob and the associate pastors at Archangel. He was pleased, but not surprised, when it did not come up as he personally handled Marco and Michelle's premarital counseling.

Michelle was looking forward to their wedding night. Things with Marco on the physical side had picked up the past few months, and they were making out regularly and he occasionally touched her breasts. She also sometimes felt something hard under his jeans. Marco for his part was optimistic that he was ready for a peak performance after years of diligent training with The Program.

In the bridal suite he used techniques he had seen in one of the very few R-rated movies he had watched. He slowly undressed Michelle and caressed every sensitive part of her body. As he undressed her, he saw that she was better built and more attractive than any of the 1950s pin-ups he had ever laid eyes on and he was able to get hard. She was clearly aroused and he entered her but was soft almost as soon as it began.

Michelle was understanding and figured that it must have been nerves.

15. Why Men Stray

Marco stayed nervous and Michelle remained understanding all summer long. She was also busy studying for the bar exam and doing legal research for Dean Moon, who was working on a book about the concept of original intent as it applied to the U.S. Constitution. Moon hoped to explain how issues like slavery and the Three-Fifths Compromise were not part of the original intent of the framers. Marco was equally busy expanding the suite of counseling services offered to the Archangel community.

In early September, Pastor Bob gave a sermon—one of his best—on "Why Men Stray." He was motivated to cover this topic based on his observations along with rumors that more adultery cases were occurring in the Archangel congregation. In the sermon he outlined how it was the wife's duty to prevent men from straying by keeping their husband's "animalistic urges tamed." To do this successfully, "a wife needed to remain attractive to her husband, to please him, to obey him, and to service—I mean, serve—him in every imaginable way."

The sermon was a big hit and ultimately the basis of Pastor Bob's first best seller *Why Men Stray.* It also generated increased attendance by women at the Archangel Christian Church Wellness Center (ACCWC). Demand for weight loss programing at the ACCWC also increased.

The Why Men Stray sermon also empowered Michelle to have a heart-to-heart with Marco about "what am I doing wrong, and what can I do differently?" Marco partially confessed about his unnatural urges and shared some of the classic pin-up magazines in his collection with Michelle.

In an effort to tame (or perhaps awaken) Marco's animalistic urges, Michelle obtained a riding crop, some rope, and leather underwear. She did her best. Through trial and error, Michelle and Marco found that if she tied him face up on their bed blindfolded, with his arms extended and ankles bound, he could usually become semi-aroused. With a few careful strokes of the riding crop, his arousal would increase. By using her mouth she could finish him. Because they wanted children, she experimented with straddling and mounting him right before he finished. She was able to do this quickly because of her tremendous abdominal strength and overall high level of physical conditioning.

Using these mechanics, she was occasionally successful in capturing his seed. However, she was unsuccessful in getting pregnant.

Any satisfaction she obtained was still obtained in the shower. While this was frustrating, it did have the benefit of keeping her doing thousands of sit-ups per week.

16. The First Moon Investigation

The details of the first Moon Investigation and *Moon Report* are well known. By the mid-1990s, allegations that in the 1980s President and Mrs. McClintock had been involved in a shady real estate deal when he was governor of Tennessee could no longer be ignored. The deal centered on property that would become lakefront due to the damming of the Cahulawassee River as it crossed from Tennessee into Georgia.

Prior to serving as 42nd President, William (Willie) Jackson McClintock had been governor of Tennessee from 1980-1988. He was born poor in Nashville to a single mother and attended the University of Tennessee, was a Rhodes Scholar, and then went to law school at Yale (where he met his future wife Beth). Outside of the events uncovered by the Moon Investigation, McClintock's time in office was marked by an impressive array of policy achievements and a strong economy. His support among African Americans was especially impressive, and he was sometimes called "the first black president." McClintock is widely regarded as the last great "retail politician" by scholars of the U.S. presidency.

Because as a McClintock appointee she was conflicted, Attorney General Jane Elko appointed Archangel Law School Dean Art Moon as a special counsel to investigate the matter. Moon had an excellent reputation as a former federal judge, and although conservative, he was not a fire-breather in public. He took a leave of absence from his position as dean of the Archangel Law School.

The investigation of the real estate deal did not turn up much, but during the probe it became clear that President McClintock enjoyed an active and varied sex life in the Oval Office. When being deposed about his interactions with a White House intern, he said, "I did not have sex with that woman." Semen stains were found on the Presidential Seal woven into the carpet of the Oval Office. Clearly, McClintock had in fact had sex with "that woman."

All of this was detailed in the first *Moon Report*, and as a result McClintock was ultimately impeached for lying during the investigation. He was not convicted.

Lesser known is the role that Michelle Pailer played in all of this. She had joined the Moon team as it investigated President McClintock and was actually present when McClintock was deposed. As the most junior and least experienced attorney on the Moon team, she was surprised to be involved in the actual interview. She was even more surprised when Judge Moon gave her detailed instructions about what to wear to the interview, including emphasizing several times that she needed to wear a low-cut blouse with her conservative dark gray business suit. He gently explained to her that President McClintock was easily distracted by attractive women. He hoped, he said, that her presence at the interview would keep McClintock from "staying focused" and prevent him from "getting crafty" while under oath.

The strategy worked, and McClintock was staring right at her when he was asked about sex in the Oval Office. He was in fact so distracted by Michelle's chest that when Moon asked the "sex with" question, a confused McClintock thought it was about Michelle whom he had never seen before that day.

17. The Twins: Boris & Vladislav

Both Michelle and Judge Moon returned to Archangel Law School full-time in the summer of 1997, and she continued to work as his primary research assistant and draft writer. He was a generous boss. His legal books and memoirs of the Moon Investigation sold well, and Michelle was justly compensated.

Despite ramping up The Program to maximal tolerable settings and extreme levels of obedience by Michelle, the Pailers were unable to conceive. Fortunately, Faith Gerald had been working with a program to place Russian orphans with barren Christian couples like the Pailers. When the opportunity came to place adorable healthy infant twin boys from Omsk, she jumped at this blessing for the Pailers. Omsk is located in Siberia, and Faith also reasoned that the boys would be genetically preadapted to the cold and likely to thrive in Minnesota.

The boys were named Boris and Vladislav. They arrived in Minnesota with Faith on December 25, 1997, the day they turned nine months old. The Pailers and the entire Archangel community were thrilled. For Marco, the pressure to perform was finally off.

The twins were not only healthy, they were hyperhealthy. They walked early, could climb almost anything, and were unusually well muscled for toddlers. It was, as Faith Gerald had predicted, like they had been bred for a life in Minnesota. Two Christmases later, Grandpa Bruce gave them both skates and sawed-off hockey sticks. By the time the small ice rink that Grandpa Bruce had set up in the Jensen backyard melted in mid-March of 2000, both of the twins could shoot biomechanically perfect, accurate, and high-velocity slap shots. They would be three in a couple weeks. That summer they took to golf and baseball with the same ease.

The only real challenge for the Pailers in 2000 was when Judge Moon was named president of his alma mater, Briles Baptist University. However, it turned out to be another blessing in disguise. Moon intended to keep writing books and articles while at Briles and suggested that he and Michelle could continue their collaboration remotely.

The Briles Baptist University trustees were thrilled that a dynamic voice of the Christian legal community was taking over. That he was an alumnus who understood the mission and values of Briles was even better. They were more than supportive when it came to underwriting his "lay ministry," which included writing books and articles along with public lectures. A state-of-the-art TV studio was constructed next to the president's office at Briles to facilitate appearances by Moon on cable TV.

The trustees were also more than happy to put Michelle Pailer on the Briles payroll, cover the cost of any long-distance calls, and install a high-end fax machine and computer with a modem at her home office. Because the twins shared a bedroom at their new home in the Twin Cities suburb of Lews, Minnesota, Michelle was able to convert one of the unused bedroom into a home office. As Internet technology improved rapidly in the 2000s, Briles IT professionals made sure she always had the most recent upgrades.

Lews was an outer ring suburb of recently converted farmland. The schools were thought to be good, and it was possible for a young family with two incomes and children to purchase a big house there. A Lews home was typically on a large lot and included four bedrooms with a master bedroom suite, three bathrooms, a finished basement, and a spacious three car garage. Nearby amenities included plenty of parks, bike trails, and a new championship golf course. There was also easy access to nearby freeways.

18. Growth of *The Program*

The National Center for Gender Confusion experienced low-key but explosive growth in the 2000s. Recruitment of new "clients" was by word of mouth or referral by a pastor. The Center's Internet and electronic footprints were kept minimal to avoid controversy and prevent the Center from being outed by the worldwide homosexual conspiracy.

The do-it-yourself flash card and stimulator system originally developed by Marco was modernized, miniaturized, and professionalized. This had the advantage of allowing clients to discreetly use the stimulator under almost any circumstances that might evoke unwanted, unnatural urges, for example at the beach or in the gym.

One of the big successes for the Center was Archangel Christian Church music director Baker Jimerson. He had used The Program successfully, and except for a few after-hours encounters with Marco in the Archangel Christian Church Wellness Center sauna, he had been mostly interested in women. This allowed him to marry one of the children's music staff members, and they were gifted with children right away. Incredibly for Marco, the after-hours sauna encounters with Baker were his only overt failures with The Program since he had developed it in the late 1980s. He experienced extreme guilt about the Baker incidents, but at the same time his overall success with The Program was validating.

19. 2000-2010: Two Mommies

As the 2000s progressed, life for the Pailers seemed idyllic, and both Michelle and Marco had adapted to their unusual approach to marital relations. They had an extensive home gym in their large heated garage where they enjoyed spending time working out together and doing set after set of sit-ups. The twins started to join them when they were about four years old. In no time, they were doing multiple sets of push-ups and pull-ups on the custom equipment that Grandpa Bruce had built for them in his shop and installed in the Pailer garage. The twins learned to jump rope and juggle and could ride bikes before age five. They had mastered the unicycle by age six.

The twins started school at Howe Elementary. The Pailers had considered homeschooling, but Michelle was too busy working remotely for Art Moon and Briles Baptist University. They figured that attending public school was low risk as long as they stayed vigilant. Alarms were raised when Pastor Bob, in one of his family values themed sermons, read a list of school districts in the Twin Cities metro area that had copies of *Heather Has Two Mommies* in their libraries. Lews was on the list.

Michelle looked into it further and found there were all sorts of problematic books on the shelves of the libraries in the Lews School District. The situation got worse when she learned that the twins' best friends at school, another set of twins and the only boys who could keep up with them on the playground, had two mommies.

Michelle and Marco prayed about it and they consulted Pastor Bob. Pastor Bob said that this was an opportunity. An opportunity to use her legal training to get "more involved" with the Lews School Board. He encouraged her to let her twins play with the other twins so that these boys had a model of a "biblically correct family unit." Their example, he said, might buffer "any indoctrination" the second set of twins were receiving from "their so-called mothers, and the radical lesbian feminist community more generally."

Michelle started attending school board meetings and alerting like-minded people in Lews about the situation. They had limited success in changing much, so—with the encouragement of Marco and blessing of Pastor Bob—she ran for the school board in 2006. It was a low turnout election, and with the help of an intensive voter mobilization effort by faith-based organizations, a conservative majority was elected to the Lews School Board. The new majority was only partially successful in cleaning up the libraries and limiting the books read in high school English classes. They worked to make sure that Creation Science was given equal time with Darwinism. An "abstinence-only" focus was also implemented in junior high and high school health classes. After consulting with Judge Moon, who told her that prayer in public school was settled law and probably a bridge too far, Michelle and her school board team focused instead on making sure faith-based after school clubs were welcome at Lews High School.

Tammy Mulkey, an attorney and the executive director of the Minnesota ACLU, was also a Lews resident. She fought the Pailer agenda every step of the way. She loved Boris and Vladislav and hoped that she and her partner Helen Jones, along with their twin boys Wayne and Bobby, could show the Pailer twins a more accepting way to view the world.

20. The Minnesota House

The Pailers lived in a suburban Minnesota legislative district that had been gerrymandered to favor Republican candidates. In 2006, Michelle decided to take "the fight for family values to the State House." She easily won the nomination and general election. There she pursued an agenda identical to the one she had on the Lews School Board, with the addition of supporting efforts to restrict abortion. Most of the initiatives she was interested in went nowhere. She was reelected in 2008 but this time by a razor-thin margin.

Michelle's increasing political commitments and the growth of Marco's National Center for Gender Confusion meant that both of the Pailers were almost too busy to be good parents. Fortunately for Boris and Vladislav, Grandpa Bruce had retired from his position as Associate Athletic Director at the University of Minnesota. Both he and Kaye were available to take the boys to sports practice and make sure someone was always available to drive them to their seemingly endless elite youth sports traveling team games. On days without formal practice, Grandpa Bruce taught the boys old-school drills using things like traffic cones to further improve their natural agility. He also installed a 45-foot rope for them to climb on the big tree in his backyard.

A few years earlier, Grandpa Bruce had seen the Jones-Mulkey twins climbing on the jungle gym at a park in Lews. Based on his years as a coach and athletic administrator, he could spot raw athletic talent when he saw it, and these boys clearly had plenty. Bruce Jensen was a low-key man, and Tammy knew him from her days as a world-class javelin thrower. His deep Scandinavian Lutheran faith, along with his experiences with all sorts of people over the years, had made him accepting of everyone. Over the next few years, Bruce gained the trust of Tammy and Helen, and their twins started playing on the same teams as Boris and Vladislav.

The elite youth sports teams the four boys played on as they got older dominated the competition. People who knew about the differing family dynamics of the two sets of twins generally kept their mouths shut. It wasn't until years later when all four boys were starting for the University of Minnesota Gopher Hockey Team that anyone tried to make an issue of it. By then, the Gophers were once again dominating college hockey and no one cared.

Boris and Vladislav were generally uninterested about anything that was happening at Archangel Christian Church, and they could be disruptive when they attended. At age 11, for example, after services one Sunday as the congregation was in line to shake hands with Pastor Bob, they spontaneously scaled the large modernistic cross in the sanctuary and engaged in an impromptu pull-up competition. The twins were incredibly strong from rope climbing in the tree at Grandpa's house, so they were up there for a while. It was the final straw.

Fortunately for everyone involved, the twins were spending so much time at their grandparents' home and on traveling teams with Sunday games, their attendance at Archangel Sunday services was spotty. After conferring with Pastor Bob, who was also concerned about what the twins might do next, their parents allowed them to skip most weekends provided Grandpa Bruce promised to take them to church someplace every weekend, which he did without fail.

Pastor Bob predicted the twins would "come back to the authentic church when they were ready."

With the twins mostly out of her hair, Michelle could fully focus her energies on further promoting family values in Minnesota.

21. 2010-2013: Carlos "Mr. Biceps" Coronado

The 2010 election in Minnesota was expected to be a blowout contest between the presumptive Democratic Farmer Labor party nominee, Minnesota Secretary of State Floyd B. (Skipper) Olson IV, and whatever generic Republican was nominated. Things were headed in that direction until a "draft Pailer" movement started in the early summer and she unexpectedly received the nonbinding Republican endorsement at the state convention. She electrified the convention when she said her mission was to "make Minnesota safe for family values." The primary turnout was predictably low. However, the highly motivated and well-organized "Christian values voters" showed up, and Pailer had the Republican gubernatorial nomination.

Skipper Olson was expected to win in something bigger than a blowout.

However, earlier in the summer the Non Aligned Party had nominated Carlos Coronado to be their candidate. Coronado was born Carl Corteso and had grown up in the Upper Peninsula of Michigan, where his father worked as a miner. After graduating from Iron Mountain High School where he excelled in sports, he joined the U.S. Navy. Corteso was extremely fit and successfully completed Navy SEAL training. After eight years in the Navy, he declined to reenlist and moved to Venice, California, in the early 1980s. He made good money working as a bouncer at night and enjoyed spending his days working out with weights on Muscle Beach.

After a few months at Muscle Beach, Corteso was spotted by a professional wrestling scout who felt that his back story as a SEAL "would work" in professional wrestling. The scout suggested the stage name Carlos Coronado after the SEAL base near San Diego and sent him to wrestling school (there is such a thing), where he learned to fake fight and jump off turnbuckles. Coronado started using anabolic steroids, and his physique went from impressive to really impressive— especially his arms. Within a couple of years, he was a major star in the IWA, the wrestling circuit owned by Richard Schrimpf, and was known as Carlos "Mr. Biceps" Coronado. Action films followed, and by the mid-1990s he was a rich man with an aching body who knew he needed to go off steroids. He was married with a couple of teenage kids and wanted to get out of California. So he moved the family to Minnesota, where he could be closer to his extended family, snowmobile in the winter, fish in the summer, hunt in the fall, and serve as a volunteer coach for his son's sports teams.

All of this was fine but pretty boring for Coronado, and then luck struck again. In the lead-up to a WrestleMaxia event at the Metrodome, he was invited to appear on a local talk radio program, which was really entertaining and enjoyable. The station manager asked if he was interested in a regular gig, and within a few months Carlos Coronado was, to put it in his words, "crushing the ratings." As talk radio became more political, Coronado offered small government and libertarian ad lib takes on various things, skewered hypocrisy in the political class, and as one columnist said, perfected "the concept of F-off as a political philosophy."

His goal in running for the Non Aligned Party nomination was to get on the ticket, expand his brand, and generate more material for his radio program, which he hoped to go national within the next year or two.

This was a great plan except that Coronado's poll numbers were surprisingly good. When he started polling at over 15%, he was invited to televised debates all over Minnesota, where he again "crushed it." Skipper Olson was a boring guy, and even though he had detailed and common sense policy ideas and a lot of experience, when it came to the media he was out of his league compared to Coronado. Pailer also performed very well on TV, and the visual of short stumpy Olson between the towering and still buff Coronado and the extremely attractive and well-spoken Pailer was too much. On election day, Pailer got the anticipated 37% of the vote, Olson got 35%, and Coronado pulled in an amazing 28%.

Pailer ran better than expected in the heavily Democratic Iron Range of northern Minnesota when she promised to pursue a policy of "dig, baby, dig." She also appealed to socially conservative voters in outstate Minnesota. Many of these folks wondered what the hell was going on down in Minneapolis, where sightings of men holding hands with men and women with women had been reported on the campus of the University.

Meanwhile, Tammy Mulkey, the executive director of the Minnesota ACLU and Pailer's opponent on the "Two Mommies" book issue in Lews, was elected attorney general. Michelle Pailer's older brother

Steve, a successful orthopedic surgeon in the suburbs, cut a pro-Olson ad in which he said, "I love my sister, but I would never vote for her."

Within a couple of months, Coronado had a nationally syndicated radio show that was crushing the ratings.

22. The Pailer Agenda

True to her word, Pailer pursued a series of socially conservative scorched-earth policies. They went nowhere, and Attorney General Mulkey and the Obama Administration were able to block essentially all of them. The press also—using the most lurid printable terms—started, in Michelle's words, "to unfairly target the good work my husband is doing with young men suffering from gender confusion issues." The publicity increased referrals from concerned parents all over the country, and demand for services at the Center was higher than ever.

To all but her base, Pailer was politically radioactive, and barring another run by Coronado, there was no way she would ever be reelected. Coronado had now gone "totally national," and he simply said that if he ever ran for office again, it would be "to live in the big house at 1600 P-A Ave."

23. The Big C or Marco's Urges Finally Go Away

As a member of the hierarchy of the Archangel Christian organization, Marco Pailer was strongly encouraged to get regular physical exams. When he turned 50 in 2012, he got the recommended colonoscopy and prostate cancer screening. His PSA blood test came back highly elevated. This led to a biopsy and the diagnosis of an aggressive, testosterone-sensitive form of prostate cancer. Marco was told that with a robotic, nerve-sparing surgical procedure, his chances of both cure and good post-op sexual function were reasonable. However, he would have to undergo a period of hormonal deprivation therapy for months following the operation. The good news, his surgeon told him, was that while his cancer was aggressive the fact that it was hormone sensitive was a positive sign and typically associated with "prolonged survival."

The operation itself was unremarkable, but the surgical nurse who placed Marco's urinary catheter wondered if he simply had an unusually pigmented penis or if the strange colors and what looked like scar tissue were from a fire or something. He also noted to himself that Pailer had unusually tight abs for a 50-year-old man.

The privacy of the Pailer family was respected by the media, and except for some idle gossip in the medical community, nothing leaked.

Marco Pailer recovered quickly from surgery and his urinary catheter was out in a few days, but within a few weeks hot flashes from the hormone deprivation therapy started to occur. He noticed that his stamina was down, he was eating more, and his tight abs were fading. He was also losing muscle tone. He hoped he could reverse these physical changes when he was able to start working out again six weeks after surgery.

One positive effect of the surgery and hormone deprivation therapy for Marco was when he returned to work at the National Center for Gender Confusion, he no longer felt a sensation of fullness in his loins when he interacted with his well-groomed younger male colleagues or provided continuing education on the latest updates to The Program. For the first time in more than 25 years he was not excited when personally counseling young men who suffered from the Gender Confusion Syndrome. He went weeks without the need for a personal application of The Program, and he had no need for corporal punishment from Michelle.

Without his hormones and the extra sit-ups, Marco grew flabby and his muscle tone continued to fall. As difficult as that was, the end of the urges perhaps was another blessing in disguise. He thanked the Lord that the urges finally seemed under control.

Over the next few years, efforts were made to wean Marco off the hormone deprivation drugs, but each time his PSA level increased and (much to his relief) the hormone deprivation drugs were restarted.

24. 2013-2016: More Time With Marco & My Family

By late 2013, it was clear that Michelle Pailer was perhaps the most polarizing and least popular political figure in the history of the state of Minnesota. A Minnesota Public Radio/*Minneapolis Star Tribune* poll had her approval rating at less than 30%. Internal Republican Party polling was equally dire if not worse. The business community in the Twin Cities was actively seeking someone to challenge her for the Republican nomination, fearing that all the talk about "family values" was hurting convention business. There was even talk that the 2018 Super Bowl might be moved. Her husband's health was a concern, although she did appreciate taking a break from the corporal aspects of their relationship. To be truthful, she did not enjoy it *that much*. Because she too was doing fewer sit-ups than at any time since she first saw Marco in the Archangel College weight room, she paid special attention to what she ate and incorporated more abdominal work into her regular exercise routine.

Since turning 16 years old, Michelle had frequently sought the advice of Pastor Bob when confronted by life challenges. Pastor Bob was spending more and more time away from the Archangel campus as his ministry gained international stature, but she was able to schedule a 45-minute block of time to visit with him in early January of 2014. Michelle told Pastor Bob that her heart was no longer in being governor, she was worried about Marco's health, and she was concerned that without Marco's income they would have a hard time "living the way we want to live in the Twin Cities."

Pastor Bob was reassuring and explained that this was simply the Lord providing new opportunities for the Pailer family. He said that one of Marco's many well-trained and dynamic protégés could easily take over as leader of the Center and that Marco would have a generous transition and retirement package. He asked if she was interested in speaking "all over America at places like Archangel." He explained that he had more speaking offers than he could ever accept, the honoraria were "extremely generous," and that she was a natural. He also mentioned that the popular Voice of Archangel satellite radio station was looking for a morning hostess.

Pastor Bob's advice was that, based on the opportunities they had discussed, the time was right for Michelle "to point her public ministry in a new direction." She discussed Pastor Bob's ideas with Marco and the next week announced that she was not going to seek reelection as governor of the State of Minnesota. She immediately signed a deal with Pastor Bob's "public appearance consultant" who would arrange speaking and other opportunities for her, coordinate travel, and look for opportunities to write books and appear on cable TV.

The opportunities outlined by Pastor Bob worked out better than planned. Michelle had a number of appearances booked prior to leaving office. By early 2015, she was speaking once or twice a week to big crowds and happily accepting the extremely generous honoraria that came with each appearance. Her radio show was a hit, and in the summer of 2015 the "Michelle Pailer Asks" 30-minute interview show was launched on Archangel TV. The show was so popular that within a few months it was acquired by Fox News and debuted to a national audience in early 2016.

Michelle interviewed all of the Republican presidential candidates and found most of them low energy and boring. Only Richard Schrimpf had any "it." When they chatted on her show, Michelle wore the same type of low-cut blouse she had worn as a young lawyer many years ago when she was working with Judge Moon investigating misconduct by then President Willie McClintock. While McClintock was better looking and more articulate than Schrimpf, he had also been understandably anxious. However, Schrimpf's ability to stay focused on her chest was even more impressive than she remembered McClintock's had been.

Michelle asked Schrimpf "softball" questions about trade, the border, and health care and Schrimpf gave overblown answers about his "stupendous" plans to fix them. He also pledged to protect the religious freedom of God-fearing Christians, promote school choice, and appoint judges who would not legislate from the bench. He said that the country was importing far too much semiprecious metal and that he, like she had as governor, favored a "dig, baby, dig" policy to rectify the problem. Strip mines, he said, "look great from the window of my plane."

25. 2016: Michelle Defends

At the beginning of this book, the 2016 scenario that led to the Schrimpf/Pailer victory was outlined, and there is only one more detail to add. Perhaps the most helpful thing Michelle Pailer did was defend Schrimpf in the midst of rumors (and perhaps a video) that surfaced late in the campaign about persistent serial sexual impropriety between Schrimpf and members of the Beverage Cart Brigade of well-built women who worked at his golf courses. Pailer simply and repeatedly said, "I have been around Richard Schrimpf at length for the past six months and seen him in the presence of many attractive women. He has always been attentive and a perfect gentleman." The press and many older women interpreted this to mean "I'm plenty good-looking and he has never hit on me in a serious way." The gentleman characterization aside, attentive was an understatement.

Democrats and various feminist groups denied the significance of Pailer being the first woman elected Vice President, saying she was just more proof that the patriarchy was alive and well. For her part, Pailer played down the trailblazer narrative.

26. The Worst Job Ever

The vice presidency was clearly the worst job Michelle Pailer had ever had. The White House kept her out of the public eye as much as possible. Except for safe appearances in front of her base and attending meaningless foreign events like state funerals, she did not do much. She also missed the Archangel community and found life in the Vice President's Residence confining. She could not, for example, go shopping or go for a jog around the National Mall without a major production being required.

Anything she did say was highly scripted. She rarely saw President Schrimpf, except for the weekly hamburger and Diet Dr. Pepper date for lunch at the White House. The President typically jumped from one topic to another, riffing on what he had seen on cable TV news over the last 24 hours, or he stared at her chest.

Marco, wanting nothing to do with the "cesspool of Washington," had remained in Minnesota, continuing to mostly fundraise in his Director Emeritus position at the Center. The twins were busy, along with the Jones-Mulkey twins, leading the University of Minnesota Hockey Team to serial NCAA championships. They were dubbed "Team 2-squared." Hockey fans all over the state knew that the glory days of both winning and Herb Brooks–style creative hockey were back. The four of them and their teammates leveraged exceptional conditioning, superior skating, accurate passing, and constant movement to create angles and open shots. They dominated the competition. Grandpa Bruce had seen it coming and was not surprised.

Michelle's only outlet for her energy was the recently refurbished state-of-the-art gym on the roof of the VP's Residence. She could not help but notice Andy Jeffs, who was one of the Secret Service agents assigned to protect her. Jeffs was in his early 40s, and Michelle had never seen a man who looked better in a black suit.

Jeffs had grown up in Chandler, Arizona. In 1992, he was recruited as a promising pole-vaulter by the Hall of Fame track coach Murray Davis at the University of Arizona located in Tucson (90 miles south of Chandler). When Jeffs got to campus, Coach Davis noted immediately that he could do just about anything athletically and encouraged him to try the 10-event decathlon. Jeffs scored an impressive 7,423 points in his first try in the spring of 1993 and from then on shifted his focus to the decathlon. Within a couple of years, he was breaking 8,000s points and considered world class.

At Arizona, in addition to his athletic success, Jeffs also had a hard time keeping women away. His impressive physique was made even more attractive by regularly sunbathing naked on the upper deck of the empty Arizona Stadium. He once missed a team plane back from the West Coast because he was apparently being "held hostage," as he later explained to Coach Davis, by a crew of female flight attendants.

After an unexpected bronze medal performance at the 1996 Olympics at age 22, he was widely considered one of the favorites for gold in 2000. Unfortunately, his pole broke during the 2000 Olympic Trials, ending his chances to win at Sydney. Nagging hamstring problems forced him to retire from competition a few years later. However, he continued to train like a madman and still weighed 209 pounds, which was still perfectly distributed over his 6'-2" frame.

Jeffs joined the Secret Service in the mid-2000s. He spent the first 10 years of his career on various interagency task forces focused on eliminating the black market for anabolic steroids and other performance-enhancing drugs used by elite athletes. As a clean athlete who resented dopers, this was his mission.

Over the years, his frustration with various governing bodies and professional leagues grew. Jeffs began to believe that they had no interest in truly solving the drug problem in sports. When he was accused of leaking information to the press, he simply responded to his supervisors, "You can fire me, but you can't execute me." Unwilling to risk the fallout from firing a high-profile agent like Jeffs, he was transferred to the protective arm of the Secret Service.

The stress of his work investigating performance-enhancing drugs also led to a divorce. Jeffs had no children. His current social situation was unknown.

Vice President Pailer learned about Agent Jeffs' background and began asking him for tips she could use in her daily workouts. Eventually she invited him to the gym to demonstrate some of the techniques they had discussed. His first lesson was that he never "worked out," he *trained*. He then explained the difference. "Working out is mindless," he said to the Vice President, "training is purposeful and goal-directed."

Over time, Jeffs redesigned and simplified Michelle's strength-training routine in a way that actually added muscle mass to the 49-year-old Vice President. The VP was thrilled because among other things, she was concerned about the potential effects of menopause on her body composition and had recently started using an estrogen patch. Jeffs also instructed the Vice President to drink a high-protein smoothie immediately after training. The simplified routine included a cycle of hard and easy training days, and he frequently reminded Michelle, "that in order to be a maximalist, you must first be a minimalist."

Many days Michelle spent extra time in the shower after exercising with Agent Jeffs.

Jeffs eventually told her about how when he was preparing for the Olympics he had used alternating classic cuts from KC & the Sunshine Band and Barry White to help him control the tempo of his training. Faster and more intense efforts were performed during KC & the Sunshine Band cuts, with recovery and stretching during the Barry White songs. Michelle then programed selections by each artist on her Cassandra by SIREN digital assistant and music station prior to their next training session.

The addition of the music was too much, and Michelle had to have him. When her sports bra failed to contain her early one morning, he knew what to do. When she asked him later if he was worried about what happened, Jeffs simply said, "No, they can fire me, but they can't execute me." When she saw him naked that day, she thought of the Steve Reeves photos she had seen many years ago when Marco explained The Program to her. Andy Jeffs looked way better.

The Vice President tried to control herself, but she continued to train regularly with Agent Jeffs and found her showers getting shorter but her sit-up program continuing. During rare moments of reflection about the new-found intensity of her training sessions with Agent Jeffs, Michelle wondered if the examples from some of the Old Testament leaders being applied to President Schrimpf also applied to her. She was not into thinking about double standards and moved on. Over time she did, however, find her discipline about extra sit-ups declining as her training time with Agent Jeffs increased.

She made a couple of other attempts to further discuss what was happening with Jeffs and asked why he never hesitated with her.

"Sweetheart," he said, "you can't jump a wide chasm in two leaps." No one had ever called her sweetheart before.

27. 2020-2022: The Decline of President Schrimpf

After winning reelection in 2020, Richard Schrimpf was bored. The media started to pay less attention to him. When internal Fox News polling showed he couldn't generate the numbers he once did, they started to turn on him and point out how he had failed to deliver on most of his promises. It was a boon for their ratings. CNN started to defend him. Go figure, but as one senior Fox executive was fond of saying, "People get bored—even *Charlie's Angels* eventually went off the air."

As a result of his deep boredom, President Schrimpf spent less and less time in Washington and more time at his golf courses.

The golf courses weren't as fun as they used to be. The constant scrutiny and security around him made it impossible for him to spend time alone with one or more of his favorite beverage cart drivers. Worse yet, due to warm water in the Atlantic, the weather in Florida had been unusually erratic for a few years. Many of his Florida golf courses were flooded from time to time and salt water was bad for the greens, so when it was cold in Washington he had to spend more and more time at his course on the Gulf Coast of Alabama.

The Links at Gulf Strand was a nice course but not Florida. The drive from the Pensacola Naval Air Station to the course was longer than the drive in Florida, and even the presidential motorcade was slowed by the checkpoint for illegal immigrants at the Florida-Alabama border. The checkpoint idea was Schrimpf's. He had them instituted at every major state-to-state border crossing. The idea was widely popular with his base until traffic slowed down enough and the protests started. The state-to-state checkpoints were then scrapped pretty quickly, but they remained popular in Alabama, so they continued via a state initiative.

His fourth wife, Tatiana, was still highly attractive and didn't mind spending time in Alabama and she was still seen at his side as required. She remained enthusiastic about their normal sex for jewelry shopping deal. Over the years, the value of her jewelry had grown to be far greater than the limited provisions in her prenuptial agreement. The early days of the Schrimpf presidency had been especially good for the collection because due to security concerns, he basically had no other outlets. However, no matter how hard she tried and how much testosterone and Viagra the President took, his stamina was shot, and sometimes he even seemed confused. He had gained so much weight that the mechanics of sex with Schrimpf would have been challenging for any woman who was not an Olympic-caliber gymnast or committed yoga practitioner. Tatiana Schrimpf was fit and motivated, but not that fit and motivated.

The fleshy-necked Schrimpf was sleep deprived but refused to use the CPAP machine that had been prescribed to alleviate his obstructive sleep apnea. The caffeine from 10 or more Diet Dr. Peppers per day made things worse. Even playing nine holes of golf was exhausting. Since Fox had turned on him, TV news was no fun, and the only thing left to do was binge watch reruns of Hawaii 5-0 and Miami Vice. He loved to share the plot summaries with his aides, who became concerned that he thought McGarrett and Danno were real. They became even more concerned when he wondered out loud if they thought McGarrett was deserving of the Presidential Medal of Freedom. They got really concerned when he asked them to prepare a nomination and vetting packet for Steve McGarrett. Jack Lord had been dead since 1998.

He talked to his physicians. They told him the first thing he needed to do was to cut back on the Diet Dr. Peppers and use his CPAP machine. When he remembered to use his CPAP, he noticed he slept better and had a bit more energy in the morning. He started to use his CPAP more consistently, especially on the nights before he had a golf game scheduled. When he awoke on Sunday morning, April 17, 2022 (Easter by coincidence), he actually felt like playing for the first time in months. His tee time was scheduled for 10 a.m. His only partner was going to be Senator Lindsey Ritz who had become perhaps the leading Schrimpf loyalist in the Senate.

Ritz was (and remains) a long-serving Republican member of the Senate from Georgia. He was seen as a traditional conservative until partnering with Schrimpf and defending the administration on a number of policy initiatives while holding the line on corruption allegations. Ritz first came to national attention during the McClintock impeachment trial and is the only major McClintock accuser not to be engulfed in a sexual scandal of his own. He has never married and never been seen on a date.

Senator Ritz had been sent down to see President Schrimpf and assess his behavior and mental acuity at the behest of a number of cabinet members and senior senators. There were worries in Washington about Schrimpf's state of mind and mental powers. More than one behind-the-scenes discussion about the possibility of evoking the 25th Amendment and removing him from office had occurred. Many Republicans were more than willing to pull the trigger on the 25th Amendment and get someone with legislative experience like Vice President Pailer in the White House and give her a head start for 2024. This was especially true of the older senators who had no possibility of ever running for president. The Democrats were terrified of Pailer and saw her as a pleasant-speaking ideological wolf in sheep's clothing. More than one had said publicly that the only man between Michelle Pailer and White House was Richard Schrimpf.

Ritz and Schrimpf teed off at 10. Things seemed pretty normal to Ritz, with Schrimpf taking his normal share of mulligans and fudging his score. The President was ahead going into the par 5 8th hole that skirted the beach. He hit a tremendous drive aided by a sudden gust of wind off the Gulf. His second shot was perfect for the 1-iron he kept in his bag. Schrimpf had been an enthusiastic and good golfer from an early age, and he loved to hit the 1-iron—a really difficult club to play—to demonstrate his golfing prowess.

He lined up his shot and thought he had a chance to get the ball on the green for a possible eagle 3. He felt revivified for the first time in months and took a full backswing. At the top of his swing, a lightning strike from out of nowhere hit his club, followed by a single deafening thunderclap. He slumped to the ground, and the Secret Service agents and the Navy corpsman assigned to the presidential detail leapt into action.

They started CPR, got the automated defibrillator, cut his shirt off, placed the pads on Schrimpf's chest, and followed the instructions from the defibrillator's artificial voice. Schrimpf had no pulse, and his ECG was a flat line. All efforts to ventilate the President were futile, his neck and jowls were just too thick and layered with loose skin. The corpsman performed an emergency tracheostomy—like he had done many times in Afghanistan—and that helped with breathing, but repeated efforts to shock the President failed to establish a viable heart rhythm. He had no luck starting an IV in Schrimpf's fleshy arms as the Secret Service agents continued to perform CPR.

Senator Ritz dialed 911.

It took nearly 30 minutes to get the President to the fully equipped medical station in the basement of the golf course clubhouse. The Navy doctor on duty saw it was futile to continue and pronounced President Schrimpf dead at 12:32 p.m.

28. The Destroyer *Hilton*

About 10 miles off the beach, the destroyer *Hannibal D. Hilton* was on patrol. It was standard Navy practice to send a number of ships to patrol offshore whenever the President was near the water for an extended period of time. After the *USS Cole* bombing in 2000 and several war-game simulations, the intelligence community and Navy were very worried about so-called swarm attacks of small boats loaded with bombs. The water hugging the 8th hole at the Links at Gulf Strand was considered especially vulnerable. In Red Team exercises, terrorists had launched inflatable speedboats from cargo ships and attacked a hypothetical beach-hugging golf course. The result was either the killing or abduction of one or more high-value human targets.

The Secret Service, Coast Guard, and Navy wanted to put big obstacles on the beach and even mine it. However, they were overruled by the President when he, for the only time in his presidency, agreed with the National Park Service. The Park Service was worried about the impact of the mines on the sea turtles that bred on the beach. President Schrimpf was worried about the effect of barriers on the view and how they would affect future sales of beach homes. In his words, "I won't have my 8th hole looking like D-Day."

It had been a busy day on the *Hilton*. The day had started with a surprise test of a new classified "microwave shotgun" system designed to stop a swarm of airborne drones. Intelligence reports suggested that airborne drones would be used in the next adaptation of the swarm strategy. With all the talk of building a wall on the border with Mexico, it was well known in the law enforcement and intelligence communities that drug dealers were already using a highly effective improvisational version of drone swarms to smuggle more drugs than ever. Street prices had never been lower.

Things started to wind down on the *Hilton* around noon, and the crew was ready for a big Spring Lunch (it was Easter, but as the result of an ACLU suit in the late 2000s, you could no longer celebrate religious holidays on ships at sea, so it was just called Spring Lunch). As Spring Lunch was starting, the ship received the highest-level presidential threat message and immediately went to battle stations. After about an hour without any further communications, the captain called the senior chief and asked if he could figure out what was going on. The chief had an old-school boom box stowed in the ship's magazine. He retrieved it and dialed in a civilian radio station and heard the news. The President had been struck by lightning while playing golf and died. He shared the news with the captain and asked, "Skipper, how the hell did that happen? There isn't a cloud in the sky, and the weather report is clear for the next 72 hours."

29. The Oath of Office

Vice President Pailer was visiting her husband and family in the Twin Cities when President Schrimpf died. It was an hour earlier in the Midwest, and she was attending services at Archangel Christian Church. She let Pastor Bob know she was coming and slipped into the choir unnoticed for most of the service, and her choir robe provided additional camouflage. The twins were busy with the NHL playoffs and not in town.

Pastor Bob had an Archangel dream in the night that included seeing a flash of lightning. The message in the dream was not clear, but he sensed the need to rewrite his planned sermon about salvation through the sacrifice and resurrection of Jesus from death on the cross and instead deliver a stem-winder about moral decay. The sermon, while a little unusual for Easter, was outstanding as Pastor Bob predicted that the dark forces of moral decay that were now infecting America would soon be on the run. Now, more than ever, all Christians had to renew their commitment to a literal interpretation of the Bible. In addition to the standard menu about abortion, homosexuality, pornography, and evolution, he mentioned the radical environmentalist conspiracy and their goal of using the threat of "so-called global warming to return us all to the Stone Age by rolling back progress." The last hymn was *Onward Christian Soldiers* as a less than quiet nod to Vice President Pailer.

In the middle of the hymn, the lead Secret Service agent on duty, Andy Jeffs, slipped into the choir area and put his arms around the Vice President's waist. He easily lifted Michelle off the riser and whisked her into the hallway outside the sanctuary. The lighting was such and the choir and congregation at such a fever pitch that no one noticed. She noticed that his touch felt nothing like it normally did.

When they got into the hallway, Jeffs told Michelle what had happened and informed her that they were headed to the federal courthouse in Minneapolis, where she would take the oath of office. His agents would collect Marco and make sure he arrived in time for the oath of office.

Judge Tammy Mulkey was the district court judge on call and would meet them there. Judge Mulkey, as we learned earlier, was a long-time political opponent of Pailer's starting with the "Two Mommies" fight during Pailer's time on the Lews School Board. After serving as Minnesota attorney general and undermining a lot of the Pailer agenda in Minnesota, she was appointed to the federal bench by President Obama.

As soon as Marco arrived, the oath of office was administered. Both women behaved in a poised and professional manner. As President Pailer left the courthouse, Judge Mulkey said, "God help us all" under her breath. Agent Jeffs, who knew Mulkey from her time as a world-class javelin thrower, played it cool and mumbled, "No shit" as he walked out the door looking straight ahead. Jeffs loved and admired a lot about President Pailer, but he could never comprehend her politics.

The presidential party then returned to the airport and took the plane that had been Air Force Two and was now designated Air Force One back to Washington.

When asked about their mom becoming President of the United States, the twins, who were in the midst of an NHL playoff series with Montreal, simply said, "Too bad for the Pres, great news for mom, and hi to dad. For now we have to avoid distractions and stay focused on winning the Stanley Cup."
As was the case when she was elected Vice President, the Democrats and various feminist groups denied the significance of Pailer being the first woman President. One of the commentators on MSNBC said Pailer "was nothing more than an unelected stooge of the patriarchy." For her part, the new President continued to play down the trailblazer narrative.

30. Her First 15 Minutes of Fame

In Madison, Joan Dark, Ph.D., and her husband, Norman Dark, Ph.D., got up early on April 17th to take advantage of the first really nice day of the spring after a very long winter. Joan was (and remains at this writing) the Dempsey Distinguished Professor of Atmospheric Science at the University of Wisconsin, Madison. She is considered the foremost expert in the world on climate change and "flash" weather events that might or might not be occurring with greater frequency as a result of global warming. She was born in San Francisco to hippie parents who later became corporate lawyers and early tech investors. Dr. Dark attended Caltech for all of her degrees and is a member of the National Academy of Sciences. Her blog "Weird Weather" remains one of the most widely read science blogs in the world. Her first faculty position was at the University of Minnesota, and she too lived for a time in Lews, Minnesota. She has two grown children, and her husband Norm is a Professor of Agriculture at Wisconsin and one of the world's leading experts on soybeans.

The Darks' plan was to take a long bike ride around the major lakes in Madison and have a late lunch at their favorite Ethiopian restaurant on State Street. The ride was great, and when she and Norm got to State Street, the first thing they noticed was a big crowd surrounding a lone electric guitarist playing *Ding Dong! The Witch Is Dead*, Jimi Hendrix style. They also heard words that sounded like "Ding Dong Schrimpf is dead." Norm turned to her and said, "Only in Madison," and she replied, "Don't forget Berkeley." Norn laughed and said, "No kidding, sweetie."

Joan then reflexively pulled the phone out of the pocket in her Leinenkugel Beer cycling jersey to check for messages. Her phone showed numerous text and voicemail messages including ones from NPR, CNN, and University of Wisconsin Chancellor Alvarez. She called the chancellor right away. He told her what he knew about what had happened. He then asked her to get to the media center and TV studio located in the building that housed the central administration of the University as soon as possible. The media had quickly done their homework and figured out that Joan Dark "was *the* expert" on flash weather and wanted her available to discuss the lightning strike that came out of nowhere and struck President Schrimpf dead. She explained the situation to Norm and they quickly pedaled home. While Joan cleaned up, Norm made her a peanut butter and jelly sandwich and gave her a glass of milk. He then fired up the Prius and they drove to the campus media center.

Chris Goode, the University's vice president for communications and Chancellor Alvarez's chief of staff was there to greet Joan. He briefed her and reminded her to keep her comments about global warming as neutral as possible for fear of inflaming influential conservative members of the Wisconsin Legislature, the so-called Neanderthals who were always looking for reasons to stick it to the "commies in Madison." It was also important, Goode said, that she emphasize that any opinions "were her own and not those of the University." Chancellor Alvarez heard what Goode said and told her he was not that worried about the "Neanderthals." They were "on board" with his agenda for the University after last year's Rose Bowl win and the recent Final Four appearance by the Badgers in the NCAA basketball tournament. He added that he felt that University funding was secure for "at least a couple of years" and told her she did not need to hold back.

Over and over again, Professor Dark was asked about what might have happened. Over and over, she calmly explained that even modestly higher temperature gradients between bodies of water and air could generate "micro" thunderstorms with clouds appearing for a matter of seconds, discharging a big lightning strike and then disappearing. The best-studied cases, she said, were near reservoirs and lakes in the Midwest. There was also speculation that methane from big livestock operations, or perhaps energy emitted by cell phone towers, might be associated with the phenomenon.

The maps that her graduate students had generated of confirmed flash lightning events suggested a modest statistical correlation with agricultural operations and/or cell towers, but as she said over and over again, "Correlation is not causation." She was working, she added, with the Department of Defense (DOD) to understand the phenomenon—the DOD saw it as a threat to troops—and hoped that with "more time on DOD supercomputers," the data would become clearer and allow for detailed simulations and modeling. She also said that depending on the data available, it would probably be "very difficult" to understand, much less "pin down," a cause for what happened off the coast of Alabama earlier that day.

After several hours of interviews, she returned home with Norm. They called their kids, turned their cell phones off, and took the landline phone off the hook. They then split a six-pack of Leinenkugel in silence.

Norm finally said, "Schrimpf was a real asshole, but based on the old days in Lews, I am really worried about what Michelle might do next."

"So am I," said Joan. "Really worried."

31. Ding Dong! Schrimpf Is Dead

Schrimpf had more hard-core political haters than hard-core political lovers. For the next week, as memorial events surrounding the death of President Schrimpf unfolded, flash crowds of anarchists and outside agitators showed up all over D.C., singing, "Ding Dong! Schrimpf is dead, Schrimpf is dead, the bloated old Schrimpf is dead!"

Tatiana and Richie Schrimpf, the oldest of the Schrimpf children with first wife Olga, did as much of the funeral planning as they were allowed. The last President who had died in office was John Kennedy. Both Tatiana and Richie pitched a horse-drawn caisson and burial at Arlington National Cemetery similar to JFK's. They were dissuaded from both requests.

First it was explained that the Army had no caisson big enough to hold Schrimpf's oversized casket and that even if such an oversized caisson existed, they no longer had the sort of draft horses needed to pull it. Richie's suggestion of borrowing the Anheuser-Busch Clydesdales was quickly shot down. The logistics of getting the massive horses from St. Louis to D.C. in time, and the need for specialized harnesses that were compatible with Army caissons, made it impossible.

Next, Secretary of Defense Conee pointed out that Schrimpf's history of draft deferrals for flat feet during the Vietnam era made burial at Arlington a "nonstarter." President Pailer agreed with the Secretary when after personally polling members of the Joint Chiefs of Staff, she learned they were all ready to resign en masse over the issue.

The new President personally thought a horse-drawn caisson and burial at Arlington for the late President would be "neat" and generate the sort of TV visuals Schrimpf loved so much. In that way, it would be an especially fitting tribute to him. However, Michelle had no desire to commit political suicide during her first week on the job. She instead suggested that Schrimpf be buried, as planned, in the Greek revival mausoleum he had constructed overlooking one of his golf courses in New Jersey.

Beyond these behind-the-scenes controversies and the chants of the anarchists and outside agitators, the rest of the memorial events and funeral went well. Everyone commented about the production values of the funeral, and the loyalists were thrilled with the eulogy delivered by Sean Gibbs of Fox News.

Gibbs hit the nail on the head when he closed his eulogy by saying, "We don't always get to pick our heroes. Only God can choose those who no matter how many molds they have broken, have the internal purity of essence to protect America from the forces of evil and decay."

The final hymn was *Onward Christian Soldiers.* Schrimpf was many things, but other than his first couple of marriages, there was no evidence he had willingly been inside a church for at least three decades. That the only head of state to attend the funeral was North Korea's Kim Jong-Un was a bit of a downer, and Richie's comment that the crowds were bigger than those at JFK's funeral was one of the great PR mistakes in the history of U.S.—if not world—politics.

Tatiana's designer black dress and veil ensemble was a big hit.

32. Sword of the Archangel Michelle

President Pailer's experiences winning the governorship of Minnesota and the way that the Schrimpf/Pailer ticket had won in both 2016 and 2020 held many lessons for her. She knew that it was rare for one party to win three presidential elections in a row. She also knew that for an outsider candidate, like she was in 2010 and Schrimpf was in both 2016 and 2020, it would take a combination of an energized base, luck, and unforced errors (think fast food taxes) by the Democrats for her to win in 2024. She also needed to defang any internal competition from inside the Republican Party.

To defang the internal competition, she chose former Speaker of the House, and current Heritage Foundation Fellow, Ryan Albert Rand of Iowa to be her Vice President. Rand was just a few years younger than Michelle. He was an old-school Republican who wanted to use some high-sounding but deeply flawed economic reasoning to cut taxes, increase defense spending, and restrain (cut) spending on entitlement programs like Social Security and Medicare. The rationale was always presented in a positive way and included words like individual, empowerment, initiative, and unleash. Rand had retired from the House and his speakership at the end of 2018 because of his total frustration with Schrimpf and the need to generate enough cash from lobbying and consulting fees to send his teenage kids to Ivy League schools.

Since retiring from Congress, it took Rand just a few years to generate sufficient resources to cover his kids' college expenses and pay cash for a condo in Florida. So, he said yes right away to President Pailer. Rand considered Pailer a political lightweight and figured that in no time he would be the de facto president. He told the press that he was willing to "come out of the bullpen" to help the new Pailer Administration pursue his long-standing ideas "about economic empowerment and unleashing the individual creative genius of the American people through lower taxes."

He was easily confirmed as the Vice President, and Pailer promptly named him as her administration's "point person" on economic policy. Unlike most presidents who made these sorts of pronouncements, she was serious. First, she and her most ardent supporters really did not care that much about economic issues. Second, letting Rand handle it would placate "Heritage Foundation" Republicans and keep the Editorial Board of the *Wall Street Journal* and people like Grover

Norquist off her back. Third, making Rand her economic point person freed her up to focus on family values and really engage her base.

A few weeks after the funeral, she addressed a joint session of Congress. Her form-fitting dress was red with blue trim, and her blonde hair had never looked better. She was now 54 years old, and it was almost impossible to miss how trim she was around the middle and how that trimness accentuated her always impressive bustline. Menopause and middle age can be held at bay for those willing to hit the gym religiously and do enough sit-ups.

She started with a few nice words about Schrimpf and then fired both barrels:

"Let us return," she said over and over again as she called for "a new commitment to the sanctity of human life," "a new commitment to traditional family values," "a new era of prayer in public school," "a new era of respecting the flag," "a new recognition of man's dominion over the land," "a new era of school choice," "a new era of religious freedom for Christians from the tentacles of big government," and finally "a new era that again recognizes that God created earth and the people who populate it."

Some of the Republicans went nuts, others had no idea what to do. Vice President Rand did his best to not look shocked and even awed at the boldness of what he was hearing. The Democrats sat on their hands, with mouths open. Shortly after the speech, at least one member of the Democratic Caucus was admitted to the Georgetown University cardiac ICU with chest pain.

On the way out of the chamber, Vice President Rand said to 82-year-old Speaker of the House Nancy Pelosi, "Did you just hear what I heard?"

"I sure did," she replied.

Pastor Bob, who was in the Gallery, never felt prouder. The repetitive nature of the speech was a preaching technique he had used many times in his most persuasive sermons at Archangel Christian Church. He was sure that via the Holy Spirit, the new President was channeling one of his Lenten sermons from the late 2000s.

33. Winning by Losing

True to her word, the President sent proposal after proposal to Congress. She threatened a government shutdown and default on the debt limit over school choice and prayer in public schools. She walked the Congress right up to the line and settled for less than she asked for but way more than anyone ever thought possible. Schrimpf had been an undisciplined and inconsistent negotiator. She was consistent, engaged, and a master of the details. Her demeanor was always reasonable and engaging. In a stroke of brilliance, she appointed a conservative Republican—John Santini, M.D.—as Commissioner of the FDA, and he restricted access to as much birth control as he could for "safety reasons." She ordered various agencies to cut funding to any organization ever targeted for any reason by her supporters. The cuts and policies were routinely stopped in the courts, but she ran up point after point with her base for merely trying. The cases that got to the Supreme Court routinely lost 5-4 as at least one of the conservative judges, citing precedent and secretly fearing Civil War, defected.

When the International Olympic Committee threatened to move the 2028 Summer Olympics, scheduled to be hosted in Los Angeles, over LGBT rights, she responded, "Let 'em."

Vice President Rand had meeting after meeting and took call after call from Republicans who were worried (terrified was a better word) about the upcoming 2022 midterms. Rand's only response was that he was doing his best to keep the administration focused on "cutting taxes for the purpose of economic empowerment and unshackling the initiative and creativity that made America great." His friends began to wonder if there was something in the water at the White House.

No one was more worried than Senator Ritz, and he counted his blessings that he did not have to run again until 2024. Georgia was changing, and to win reelection in 2024, Ritz needed to walk a political tightrope and avoid alienating both "values voters" and the "don't tax me but I don't give a damn on social issues voters" in the Atlanta suburbs.

In the meantime, Ritz focused on his role as Chair of the Senate Intelligence Committee. He needed to tie up the loose ends of the "Macau Casino and Plastic Surgery Investigation" and clear the late President Schrimpf's name once and for all. There was simply no hard evidence that either Chinese Intel or organized crime was involved in money laundering or a "pay to play" scheme with any member of the Schrimpf organization. RIP Richard Schrimpf.

34. J.J. Engelton—Retired CIA Officer

Since Schrimpf's death, there had been speculation on Internet sites that catered to fringe "Schrimpf-istas" that his death was more than a simple one-in-a-million, act-of-God lightning strike. Russian Intel tracked those sites and did what they could to stir the pot. John James Engelton, a retired CIA officer, also tracked the sites from his home in the Virginia suburbs of D.C.

Engelton was remarried and 70 years old. He was a tall, lanky ex–chain smoker who once consumed prodigious amounts of vodka on a daily basis. He retained the early 1980s-style mustache that had been popular among CIA agents when he first joined The Agency as a junior technical support officer. He dressed like a PGA teaching professional, and when he did attend social functions he wore a brightly colored blazer. He avoided the color green, fearing that he would be punished in perpetuity by the golf gods if he ever wore an unearned green jacket. He spent his days doing consulting work at home and spent his free time playing golf or socializing with his second wife Wendy and their friends. He wintered in Florida. His ability to actually play golf had almost been destroyed by a severe case of the yips, but he recovered after meeting Wendy in the early 2010s. Engelton was fascinated by golf club technology.

Engelton had retired—or been retired—for medical reasons from the CIA. His expertise, and indeed his gift as an intelligence officer, was his ability to figure out how every new gizmo being developed in places like Silicon Valley might be weaponized by adversaries of the United States. Over the years, he had predicted things from the rise of truck bombs, cell phones as detonators, weaponized model rockets, and even the use of commercial airliners as bombs. In the 2000s, he had warned then Vice President Cheney about the hacking risks associated with next-generation Web-linked cardiac pacemakers. Cheney opted for an older model.

With so much new technology to think about and evaluate, the stress got to him. In the late 2000s, he became convinced that a terrorist group was developing an exploding driver to be planted in the golf bag of a highly ranked PGA pro. They would then remotely detonate the device inside the driver, kill the pro and his playing partners, and inflict shrapnel injuries on nearby patrons watching in the gallery. He hypothesized that a group of radical golf fans from Spain was waiting for an optimal time to use the device when top U.S. pros including Tree Tremont were paired in the same twosome or threesome. The goal of the Spaniards, he speculated, was nothing less than destroying U.S. chances in the next Ryder Cup.

When he generated a "threat memo" on the exploding driver, at first this was seen as some sort of joke. Engelton insisted there was a "high probability" of it actually happening and stuck to his guns. When he refused to recant, his supervisors reluctantly had him undergo a fitness evaluation, and he was retired for medical reasons. He simply had to go. It was not unusual for CIA employees to get a little paranoid, in fact it could be a real asset, but the driver memo was clearly over the line. At Engelton's retirement reception, he received enough vodka to last a year. He then spent a lot of time at the 24-hour driving range near his house. The yips had robbed him of the ability to play an actual round of golf, but he could still hit the driver.

Engelton did not stay retired for long.

Cook Construction Conglomerated (CCC) was a huge construction company that was founded before WW2 and grew exponentially for decades by building military bases, dams, roads, airports, power plants, and refineries during and after the war. Since 9-11, they had been generating a major revenue stream by "hardening" public buildings that were seen as soft targets for terrorists and building domed sports stadiums for NFL teams.

CCC was run by two brothers who were charter—really founding— members of the "don't tax (or regulate) me but I don't give a damn on social issues" movement. They were conveniently oblivious to the fact that most of their contracts had something to do with the government. The NFL stadiums they were building were, for example, typically government funded "in collaboration" with a billionaire owner who had threatened to move the team if a new stadium was not built. Part of the pitch typically included a highly cooked economic impact assessment showing that footing the bill for a new stadium would be an economic bonanza for the city doing the footing.

To keep the funding for public hardening and stadiums going, demand had to grow. For demand to grow, new threats and opportunities needed to be identified. Over the years, reports made public by the CIA, largely on the basis of Engelton's anonymous "emerging threats" work, had generated a lot of business. A few months after he retired, he was contacted by the nonprofit Americans for Economic Safety Foundation (AESF) about consulting. The AESF was funded by donations from the Cook brothers and was essentially a front for their political agenda of low taxes, low regulation, less social spending, more publicly financed target hardening, and construction of things like stadiums. The AESF generated white papers on the newest terrorist threats to lobby for more funding of projects that were in the CCC corporate sweet spot.

Engelton basically read and digested information sent to him by the AESF public affairs office, generated long memos, and participated as needed in background briefings for government leaders and other opinion shapers. He was well paid. When he traveled, he stayed at the best hotels and flew on a CCC corporate jet. His efforts were judged highly successful.

In 2011, a former Fox News executive named Al Deutch took over as executive director of the AESF. He saw Engelton as an underutilized asset and looked for ways to further leverage what he was doing for them. What if Engelton's memos and briefing slides were novelized, or maybe turned into a TV series or even a movie franchise? What better way to educate the public and raise concern about various threats?

Deutch pitched the idea to the Cook brothers, who approved it immediately. He then hired a team of writers who set to work on a series of J.J. Engel novels. About the same time, Engelton began to be concerned about cheap commercially available drones. In one of the first memos after the novelization initiative started, Engelton described the possibility of a drone swarm attacking an outdoor sports stadium with fragmentation devices and a massive loss of life from the ensuing stampede.

The novel *Super Bowl Swarm* was a best seller, the movie rights were sold, and Matthew McConaughey played CIA agent J.J. Engel. Engelton had wanted the part to go to Kevin Costner, but he was considered too old by the creative people. Nevertheless, he was thrilled with the movie, which became a blockbuster. More novels and movies followed with every imaginable gizmo that Engelton's fertile mind anticipated might be weaponized in the future used in plots.

The J.J. Engel franchise was also very lucrative for Engelton. On the advice of one of the writers working on the project, he had canceled his consulting contract with the AESF and instead opted for a small percentage of the J.J. Engel gross. He used the windfall to buy a condo in Fort Myers Beach, Florida. There he met a young Canadian widow (Wendy) at the local driving range. Incredibly, she got him to quit smoking, reduce his prodigious consumption of vodka, and schedule sessions with a sports psychologist. Relaxation techniques Engelton learned from the sports psychologist cured him of the yips, and for the first time in years, he could play a round, many rounds, of golf without any suicidal thoughts.

The *Super Bowl Swarm* also raised concerns in the security office at National Football League headquarters and among NFL owners. The TV networks were also worried because—ratings aside—they had no interest in broadcasting the sort of conflagration that would happen if a drone swarm really did attack a Super Bowl in progress. One network executive pointed out that it was important to remember that "J.J. Engel is a fictitious character, but unlike his exploits, there is no guarantee that law enforcement or the intelligence community could stop such an attack."

An unwritten consensus emerged that future Super Bowls would only be scheduled in domed stadiums. More importantly, the league developed a confidential plan in collaboration with the AESF and Cook Construction Conglomerated to make sure each franchise had a new domed stadium within the next 10-15 years. Only the Green Bay Packers resisted. There was no chance the Super Bowl would ever be held at Lambeau Field in tiny Green Bay, and the Packers were reluctant to give up the late season home field advantage that came by playing outdoors on the "Frozen Tundra."

An exception was made.

Negotiations in NFL cities without domed stadiums were smoother than anticipated. Opinion polling and focus groups commissioned by the AESF showed that the J.J. Engel franchise had "clearly impacted public discourse on the topic of high-security stadiums."

35. The Engelton Dossier

By the late 2010s, Engelton's work with the AESF and Cook had slowed to a trickle. They only asked for input once in a while, which was fine with him given his renewed ability to actually play a round of golf. When President Schrimpf died, Engelton was golfing with his wife on Sanibel Island and heard the news while sipping a vodka and tonic at the 19th hole. Engelton had spent enough time on the Gulf Coast to know the weather could be pretty erratic. His improved personal life, more sleep, mellowing with age, the revivification of his golf game, and moderation in his drinking had dulled his conspiratorial imagination. As he learned more, he only wondered why the President was hitting a 1-iron. He thought to himself that if the President had been hitting a modern composite hybrid he might have survived the lightning strike. Other than that, it seemed like an act of God.

Over the course of the next few months, some of Engelton's golfing buddies started talking about things they had been hearing on talk radio or seeing on the Internet. The conspiracy theory taking shape was that clandestine cells of radical environmentalists had been somehow "manipulating the weather" around the Schrimpf golf properties to send a message to reinforce "the false narrative of man-made global warming." Were they doing this on the fateful day? Did the radical environmentalists miscalculate and instead of a rainstorm or flood generate the flash lightning strike that killed President Schrimpf? What about Schrimpf's caddy—apparently an undocumented immigrant— who had handed him the 1-iron instead of the modern composite hybrid in his bag?

Engelton heard this chatter, and as suspicious and paranoid as he could be, he just did not buy it. He knew about the research from the University of Wisconsin on flash weather and felt that there was no way that a small cell of radicals could generate the sort of concentrated energy needed in the atmosphere to reliably manipulate the weather. Presidential communications were mostly via hardened fiber optic landlines from places where presidents spent a lot of time, so that ruled out some sort of accident related to high-energy radio communications. Modern TV network satellite transmission dishes were relatively low powered, and cell phone use was highly regulated in and around the president. He was skeptical.

Engelton was skeptical until August 8th, 2022 (coincidently his 71st birthday) when he found a thin medium-sized manila envelope labeled "confidential" stuffed into his golf bag as he left the grille at his home course in Virginia. The contents of the envelope were some DOD and Navy memos about "microwave shotguns" being developed to thwart drone swarms that might attack ships. They also detailed the possible location of the destroyer *Hilton* in the spring of 2020 when it had been on presidential protection duty off the coast of Alabama. There was a PDF of a scientific paper from scientists at the University of Wisconsin titled "Modeling Microwave Energy Density and Flash Lightning Strikes in North Dakota." The envelope also included a partial transcript of an extemporaneous, somewhat drunken eulogy that a high-ranking admiral had given at a private memorial gathering for the fallen war hero and former U.S. Senator Hannibal Hilton. The gathering had apparently taken place in 2018 in a private room of Blackbeard's Public House in Annapolis, Maryland, shortly after the burial of Senator Hilton on the grounds of the U.S. Naval Academy. It was apparently an emotional speech that included the phrases "may (unintelligible) God (unintelligible) Old Testament (unintelligible) the Coward-in-Chief down (unintelligible)."

It had been a long time since Engelton's CIA reflexes had been fully activated. As interesting as the material was, he found as he scanned the documents that he could not generate the sort of intense paranoia that had once been routine. However, he did drive home and start nosing around on the Internet to see what he could learn.

What he learned was pretty straightforward:
1) The Navy did in fact have a microwave shotgun research program designed to defend ships against a hypothetical drone swarm. It had been developed based on some of his late 1990s warnings about swarms and what happened in various war-game scenarios and was further stimulated by the J.J. Engel franchise. It was classified, but a general description of a hypothetical microwave shotgun to defend against drone swarms was available on the *Popular Mechanics* website.
2) The Navy was especially worried about ship-launched drone attacks on high-value human targets (read the President of the United States) who spent a lot of time in coastal areas near the beach.
3) The *Hilton* had been doing early field testing of the system.

4) Essentially all senior Navy officers resented President Schrimpf over remarks he had repeatedly made questioning Senator Hilton's heroism.

5) The University of Wisconsin data suggested that the energy from the microwave shotgun system was sufficient to trigger a lightning strike, if atmospheric conditions were otherwise conducive.

Connect dots 1-5 in the most outrageous and paranoid way and the hypothesis that one or more senior Navy officers assigned the *Hilton* to presidential protection duty. These officers then ordered a field test of the microwave shotgun system when President Schrimpf was near the beach in hopes of disabling or killing him with a lightning strike. That Schrimpf had been playing less golf than normal threw a wrench in these plans. However, when opportunity struck on Easter Sunday 2022, it was easy to justify a trial run of the microwave shotgun on the basis of vigilance testing on a holiday. Schrimpf also got his medical care from Navy doctors and a Navy corpsman had been the first responder.

What should he do with this information? Engelton had seen the leadership of his old outfit become politicized by almost six years of Schrimpf, so he was reluctant to share it with the CIA. Plus, everyone he knew had retired long ago. The FBI had been gutted by Schrimpf, and there was no one at the Bureau who would have any idea what to do with such a report.

Engelton settled on contacting Senator Ritz, a close friend of the late Senator Hilton, a lawyer in the Naval Reserve, and (his recent political fling with Schrimpf aside) a true patriot. Plus Engelton knew Ritz from the many times he had provided confidential testimony to the Senate Intelligence Committee. None of his testimony was ever leaked.

36. The Second Moon Investigation

Senator Ritz was happy to hear from "his old friend" J.J. Engelton and returned his call immediately. Engelton simply said that he had stumbled onto a "grave threat" to national security and needed to speak confidentially to Ritz. To avoid being seen at the Capital, Engelton suggested they play nine holes of golf early one morning at his club. He instructed Ritz to park at an empty Arrowmart lot and wait for him to pick him up at 5:45 a.m. for a 6:15 tee off. The rationale, Engelton explained, was that the only people staffing the club at that hour were the Hispanic groundskeepers who were unlikely to recognize Ritz, who was a familiar face in the D.C. area.

As they played, Engelton outlined what he had heard to Ritz. Ritz's only response was, "So you think the rumors are true?" Engelton responded, "Senator, I can't rule them out and the scenario, while a stretch, is plausible." They finished the nine holes undetected before 8 a.m. Engelton dropped Ritz off at the still deserted Arrowmart parking lot. Ritz went immediately to his Georgetown row house, cleaned up, and got on the secure phone that had been installed in his house when he became Chairman of the Senate Intelligence Committee.

His first call was to Attorney General George Bush III (also known as Trip). Trip Bush was the only member of the Bush clan who had defected to the "Schrimpf-istas." He had been rewarded with a slot in the Cabinet even though he was viewed as a potential mole by Schrimpf's more ardent supporters. Ritz and Bush went over the matter and concluded they should "tell the President immediately."

By the time Attorney General Bush and Senator Ritz reached the Oval Office, the online Dredge Report had posted the Blackbeard's Pub transcript and details about the activities of the *Hannibal Hilton* on April 17, 2022. President Pailer had a crisis. Senator Ritz had an opportunity to hold hearings. The election was a few months away, and there was immediate speculation in the media that if these "explosive allegations are true" they might influence the 2022 midterms.

37. 15 Minutes More

One of the first experts to testify in front of Ritz's committee was Joan Dark, Ph.D. She essentially repeated the analysis she had provided to the media on April 17th and in subsequent interviews about flash weather events. Things got tougher when Senator Thad Cross of Texas asked, "What if the *Hilton* had been closer to shore?" and "What if the energy density of the microwave shotgun had been higher than admitted to by the Navy?" Professor Dark said it was tough to respond in detail to "hypotheticals," but if the scenario Cross was describing did in fact occur, she could not "rule anything out."

The headline in the next day's *Washington Post* was:

"Professor Can't Rule Out Schrimpf Killed by *Hilton* Lightning Strike"

When various members of the Navy brass (most of whom had been at Blackbeard's Pub) were called to testify, most said they could not remember the details. A sympathetic bartender found a copy of the tab and leaked it to the *Times*, and it was clear that essentially everyone there was drunk. An anonymous Blackbeard's employee said it was the only time in the history of the establishment that they had "run out of Captain Morgan rum." The Navy looked bad, but the inability of the admirals to remember anything was more than credible.

Ritz had spent years in the Naval Reserve, and that led to allegations that he was playing "softball" with the Navy or worse yet actively involved in the cover-up of a presidential assassination. Because so many DOJ attorneys had links to the Pentagon, there were calls for an independent counsel to take over the investigation. One talk radio host said that Trip Bush needed to recuse himself because the Navy named an aircraft carrier after his grandfather, who served as the 41st President and was a decorated naval aviator in WW2.

38. The Second Moon Investigation Continues

Because she had been a staff attorney on the Moon Investigation of President McClintock, the President told Vice President Rand that a special counsel was "the way to go." When she met with Deputy Attorney General Alex Bazar, who had supervised her work on the Moon Investigation, he indicated that he was "inclined to ask his friend and mentor Judge Moon to once again step into the breach and rescue the country." President Pailer was enthusiastic about the suggestion.

Judge Moon was thrilled. His career as a leading right-wing "Guardian of the Faith" (the title of his post-McClintock memoir) had stalled out in the mid-2010s when he was involved in an extensive cover-up of "multiple dormitory violations" (rapes) by football players at Briles Baptist University in Texas.

At the suggestion of Senator Ritz, Moon hired J.J. Engelton as a consulting investigator focused on uncovering any surreptitious electronic activity or communications. Moon and the attorneys he hired were mostly electronically illiterate, and Engelton was told he would "have a free hand and a big budget." His first recruiting call was to Reggie Randall, the retired Arrowmart data-mining wizard.

Randall is widely considered the father of improved marketing via data mining. He was originally from North Dakota and spent the 1980s working at the National Security Agency. Wanting to get closer to home, in the early 1990s he went to work in the IT department of the Arrowmart megastore chain and eventually helped the company develop methods to use credit card data, shopping history, ZIP codes, and data from other sources to target ads at specific individuals and demographic groups. His best-known projects focused on identifying pregnant women and targeting them for diaper sales. The concept was to get new moms into an Arrowmart for diapers and purchases of groceries along with the higher-margin household items. The goal was to generate a loyal Arrowmart shopper for life. A private man, he was nevertheless proud when this initiative was written up in the *New York Times*. Lesser known was his highly successful effort to increase shopping by middle-aged and older men at Arrowmart based on predicting who might be getting their Viagra at one of the many low-cost Arrowmart pharmacies. The plan was to then stock the stores with other products likely to be purchased by Viagra users. As a result of bonuses he had received for his work, Randall was able to retire early, and he still winters with his wife Peggy in Fort Myers Beach.

Engelton and Randall went way back to when Randall worked for the NSA. They both had warm weather condos in Fort Myers Beach and were regular golfing partners there. They mostly talked sports when they golfed, but Engelton remembered the several times Randall had told him there "was far more granular, accurate, and real-time information in commercial electronic databases than in anything the government had." He also noted that most people reflexively signed away any privacy protection they had, and the electronic formats used by industry were ideal for mixing and matching. By comparison, the fragmented and siloed government systems were "very difficult, if not impossible, to use in a modern way."

Randall was reluctant to come out of retirement because he did not want to travel or move. However, Arrowmart had him on a significant retainer for special projects and provided him with an impressive array of hardware at both his home in Lews, Minnesota, and his condo in Fort Myers Beach. He also knew that finding out what sort of electronic crumbs a bunch of Navy admirals had been leaving around would be, as he told Engelton, "a piece of cake, just get me the names and dates of birth."

To avoid having any of their communications intercepted, Engelton and Randall agreed to exchange information in person with "hard copies only" in lavatories located at various golf courses, driving ranges, 19th holes, and golf shops. Both found excuses to spend more time in Florida and avoid any travel that would raise red flags. They agreed to resume their normal Wednesday morning golf game in Florida the week after Labor Day.

Engelton brought Randall name after name of "persons of interest," but beyond finding out things like who was drinking a lot, in debt, watching Internet porn, impotent, having an affair, gambling, or taking psych meds, he drew a blank. He cast a wide net and worked his way back several layers, focusing on at least three degrees of relationships for each person of interest. In a couple of instances, he was able to use audio information routinely recorded by the popular Cassandra by SIREN digital assistant and music station to confirm that nothing was going on. He read some interesting transcripts of things that Cassandra heard, but again nothing stuck.

The one tidbit he could not wrap his mind around was the combination of Barry White and KC & the Sunshine Band classics that the President listened to when she was Vice President and exercising in the gym at the VP's Residence. The VP's Residence was located on the grounds of the Naval Observatory in D.C.

The investigation continued.

39. Death of an Ex-President

Former President Willie McClintock died of a heart attack at age 75 in his Harlem office on October 31, 2022, while watching Fox News after a meal of barbecue had been delivered to the office. He felt safe in Harlem and sent the security folks home to trick-or-treat with their kids. The story emerged that McClintock became overstimulated when Fox presented polling data showing the Democrats winning in a wipeout and President Pailer dragging down any remaining traditional or even remotely moderate Republican candidates in the suburbs. The polling data also showed that his wife Beth was having a major positive impact in districts that Schrimpf had won in 2016 and 2020. As his heart raced with excitement, he suffered a massive heart attack and died quickly.

That was the official story.   However, his long-time aide Marsha "Rocky" Rocker had been in the office, the barbecue order included two meals, and someone had tried to use the automated external defibrillator.

Rocky Rocker looked a lot like all of the women that former President McClintock had ever been linked to. While she was highly educated (a graduate of Barnard), she had nevertheless perfected the "Ryman look" that attracted McClintock. Ryman, as in the Ryman Auditorium and the big-haired, big-lipped, and busty Grand Ole Opry female backup singers that McClintock used to watch and lust after as a teenager in Nashville. The speculation was that she had been servicing McClintock when he had the heart attack. Unlike the late President Schrimpf, the combination of Viagra and testosterone patches worked as advertised for McClintock.

The Democrats did dominate the House races, but the Republicans held onto a 50/50 split in the Senate with Vice President Rand available to break ties. More than 20 of the 50 Republican senators were over 85, and several were from states that had recently elected Democratic governors who could typically appoint replacements in the case of a death or retirement. So the odds seemed good that the Democrats might pick up a seat at some point in the next few years. The Democrats also had plenty of really old senators, but most of them were from states controlled by the Democratic Party, so they were less worried about a death in the Senate.

The funeral of former President McClintock was held on Friday, a week after the midterm elections. The lines at the Capitol to pay respects were long as people remembered the eight years of peace and prosperity along with the budget surpluses. The sex scandals were only mentioned—even on Fox News—in passing. However, the funeral service itself was poorly attended. Beyond a few older McClintock Administration alumni, only one Democrat with any sort of future, Mac Jackson who had just been elected governor of Georgia, attended. Just as McClintock had been viewed by many as the "first black president," Jackson was frequently described as a potential "black Willie McClintock" by political insiders.

Any other Democrat with a remotely viable political future avoided the funeral over concerns about the optics of paying respects to a serial womanizer like McClintock. As expected, Republicans, except for 99-year-old Henry Kissinger, stayed away.

At the end of the service, Beth McClintock slipped a sealed envelope to the rector of the National Cathedral, caught an Uber, and vanished as the organist belted out the country classic music song *The Party's Over*. During his funeral planning, the late President McClintock had personally demanded *The Party's Over* be played as the recessional. He figured it would be his last chance to poke fun at the holier-than-thou crowd that had tormented him over the years. At least one reporter looked up the lyrics of *The Party's Over* and speculated that perhaps McClintock was actually apologizing to his wife.

Mrs. McClintock's handwritten note read:

"To my family and friends, I am taking a break from public life and hope you can respect my privacy.

Sincerely,
Beth J. Campbell"

Campbell was her maiden name, Joan was her middle name. Bank records showed that for the past several years, she had made numerous large cash withdrawals.

For almost six years, there were occasional unconfirmed Beth sightings in India, Peru, Big Sur, the Shetland Islands, Boulder, Colorado, and near Taos, New Mexico. Some people thought they had seen her in

Spain doing the Pilgrimage of St. James. She was, in fact, spending most of her time near a Buddhist retreat and monastery outside Santa Fe, New Mexico. She also sought the advice of Don Juan, an old Native American medicine man who (with the aid of a bit of peyote) helped her reconcile the tremendous love and admiration she felt for her late husband with the hatred and resentment she felt over his many betrayals. She also took up aikido and, for the first time in her life, got really fit.

The few times Beth was spotted, she was always seen wearing a long black hooded robe, Ray Ban sunglasses, her hair pulled back, and no makeup. When anyone made knowing eye contact with her, she simply raised her right index finger to her mouth, did a quiet "Shhhhhh," and said, "I am not the person you are interested in." It worked, and no Beth sightings were ever confirmed. Campbell's only contact with her daughter Charlotte was an occasional note sent via untraceable, encrypted, and super-secure NeutronMail.

40. Harpooning the 2024 Election

Pailer's performance as president was essentially a repeat of what happened in Minnesota during her time as governor. She played to her base, all of her social initiatives stalled, and the only thing she accomplished was the appointment of a few conservative federal judges with the help of Senate Majority Leader Trent McDonald. That ended when McDonald had a stroke while speaking on the Senate floor during debate about gutting Obamacare. He ended up in the Neuro ICU at Bethesda Naval Medical Center in a chronic vegetative state. The provisions for replacing a disabled senator in Kentucky were obscure, the Democrats sued, and the seat remained open until 2024.

Most observers expected the Republicans to "go in a different direction" in 2024. However, the party was in such disarray, and because the "values voters" were really the only organized block, they were able to hold onto the nomination. Rand was on the ticket, which gave the rest of the party "fewer viable options." Pailer and Rand were nominated without a serious challenge and with the full support of Buck Patrick.

As expected, the Democrats had a chaotic primary season and nominating process. They settled on 36-year-old Representative Marcella Moreno de Rincon from Brooklyn as their nominee. She was a self-described socialist and champion of Medicare for all, nationalizing various industries, and taxing the rich. As more and more people lost their health insurance and income inequality continued to spike during the Schrimpf/Pailer era, these policies were truly popular. She took predictably liberal positions on all social issues and advocated developing an agency like OSHA to generate trigger warnings as needed all over the country. She supported an "absolutely open southern border." Her political reflexes were to pick a like-minded running mate to ensure that if "lightning strikes me, the movement will continue." Instead she opted to balance the ticket with the middle-aged former mayor of Phoenix, Arizona, Matt Roberts. Roberts was a successful entrepreneur who had developed a series of brew pubs connected to mountain bike stores in and around the Phoenix area. Roberts supported much of the de Rincon agenda but was lukewarm on the more socialistic elements of what she was proposing.

Mike Nemeth watched all of this in horror from his corporate offices in Portland, Oregon. Nemeth was the founder and president of Harpoon

Coffee. He was the son of Hungarian immigrants who had fled Hungary in the wake of the 1956 invasion by the Soviet Union. His father Laszlo defected at the 1956 Olympics, where he finished fourth in the 1,500-meter run. He had been one of the favorites, but his training had been interrupted by the invasion. His future wife Maria swam for Hungary and defected as well. They landed penniless in Los Angeles but ultimately built powerhouse track and swimming clubs sponsored in part by the Santa Monica Parks Department. They were also supported by the many staunch anticommunists in Southern California. Their only son Mike was born in 1958, and it was clear from the time he started walking at nine months that he had exceptional aerobic capacity. Mike was exposed to rigorous Eastern European–style physical education from an early age and saw the dedication and sacrifices made by the many great amateur athletes his parents coached.

As a senior at Santa Monica High, Mike ran 4:02 for the mile. He then enrolled at the distance running powerhouse University of Oregon on a full scholarship. He was worried that the high-intensity interval training program perfected by his father was not used at Oregon, but his dad encouraged him to give it a try and told him that he could do "all the intervals he wanted after college."

Mike Nemeth thrived at Oregon and became the top young miler in the country (if not the world), with a personal best of 3:54 as a sophomore. His grades were good, and he was considered a favorite for the U.S. team for the 1980 Olympics to be held in Moscow. His dream was to win the gold medal in Moscow and wave a Hungarian flag along with an American flag on the medal stand. He increased his training and as a junior ran 3:51:2, barely missing the American record held by the legendary Jim Ryun.

Nemeth's dreams were dashed when the U.S. boycotted the 1980 Moscow games over the Soviet invasion of Afghanistan. He continued to train for the 1984 Olympics, but a series of overuse injuries limited his competitiveness and he struggled to consistently break four minutes again.

He did, however, get a job with the emerging shoe giant Nike. Nemeth's first job was in sales up and down the West Coast. His travels frequently took him to Seattle, where he was impressed by the coffee. He thrived and caught the attention of Nike founder Phil Knight who had also run at Oregon many years before.   Knight subsequently sent him to the Stanford Graduate School of Business. His capstone project was a business plan about a national chain of "gourmet" coffee shops.

Knight asked to meet with Mike and see his business plan. When they met, Knight was impressed and told him the gourmet coffee chain was a "good idea." He staked him for $25,000 to get started in exchange for 25% of the company, which became known as Harpoon Coffee. By the early 2020s, Nemeth was worth in excess of $5 billion.

Mike Nemeth had no interest in social issues, was worried about income inequality, and thought he should be paying more taxes. He "walked the walk" by paying his employees well, providing health insurance, and developing an incentive plan for those who needed further education or training.

He was also a generally calm guy, but he thought Pailer was delusional and whenever de Rincon said the word "socialism," his blood pressure spiked. Nemeth knew all about socialism from his parents and their friends. His father Laszlo, who was sharp, fit, and active at age 96, had never been prouder of Mike.

With the planning and marketing skills he had honed as a successful businessman, Nemeth got on the ballot in almost every state and dominated the debates. The polls indicated Pailer's base was fatigued and turnout might be lower than anticipated. However, a couple of things happened. First, the idea of a trigger warning agency fired up Pailer's base. Second, they realized Pailer could not run again in 2028, and as Pastor Bob said on every media outlet he had access to, "2024 might be our community's last best hope to redeem America."

Second, audiotapes surfaced with de Rincon advocating the nationalization of college and professional sports, starting with "the billionaires who run the NFL." She said that with nationalization, it would be possible to either change the rules and make football "more like soccer" or ban the sport entirely. Most importantly, she did not back down from the comments when pressed by the media. She repeatedly called the NFL and big-time college football "nothing more than a modern-day plantation system."

Like the Big Mac fiasco of 2016, this was a gift to the Pailer/Rand ticket that allowed them to paint the Democrats as "out of touch."

Nemeth found the whole proposal inconceivable, and he had no idea how to respond.

Pailer saw the opening right away, and in her next big speech, which happened to be in Michigan, she said that "first they will come after the Detroit Lions and next it will be the University of Michigan Wolverines." Versions of that line were used all over the country and they worked.

On election day, Pailer got the anticipated 37% of the vote, de Rincon was second with 35% with Nemeth pulling in 28%. The percentages were almost identical to the 2010 gubernatorial race in Minnesota. Pailer dominated the Electoral College and won every state that had both an NFL team and/or a major college football program. This included a narrow plurality in Massachusetts, where exit polls showed the Pailer/Rand ticket getting 87% of the vote among self-described "avid" New England Patriots fans.

The Democrats picked up seats in the House and Senate and now had solid majorities in both. Pailer took solace in the conservative majority in the Supreme Court and told supporters, "Over the past 30 years, our appointment of judges who do not legislate from the bench and respect the original intent of the Constitution will serve as a firewall against the forces of moral decay." Among other things, Judge Moon's compulsory course on original intent that Michelle Pailer had taken at the Archangel School of Law in 1991 didn't cover the Three-Fifths Compromise.

41. Did Justice Cavendish Have Too Many Beers?

The summer of 2025 was both good and bad for President Pailer. A positive was that Agent Jeffs had finally been transferred from the Vice Presidential Protection Unit to the Presidential Protection Unit. This allowed them to resume their training sessions. Security was tighter in the White House than it had been at the VP's Residence, but Jeffs knew what he was up against and was able to identify gaps in the coverage that allowed him to spend alone time training with the President. These sessions, while infrequent, provided President Pailer with tremendous relief from the stresses of office and also got her back on the sit-up program that had been one of the keys to maintaining her figure over the years.

Barry White and KC & the Sunshine Band never sounded better.

On the political front, the judicial firewall took two major hits. The drugs that had kept Chief Justice Robert Johnson's multiple myeloma in check stopped working, and he stepped down to "spend more time with my wife, children, and grandchildren." Next, in August, Associate Justice Bart Cavendish died in a freak jet ski accident off the Virginia coast. He had been at a reunion of his high school basketball team and on a dare had taken a jet ski out into rough surf. The jet ski flipped, and he was not seen until his body washed up on the beach a few days later. Toxicology reports came back negative, but credit card data showed that multiple kegs of light beer had been delivered the day prior to the accident to the beach house that served as reunion headquarters. There was speculation that Cavendish had "a few beers" before taking the jet ski out, but his buddies closed ranks and denied everything.

The liberals now had a 4-3 majority on the Court that was anchored by 90-year-old Ruth Bader Ginsburg, who was still going strong. Senate Majority Leader Warren pointed out that nothing in the Constitution required nine justices and said that the "Senate would not let any president who had not received a majority of the popular vote fill a vacancy on the Court."

42. Marco Pailer Loses the Battle

Marco Pailer hated Washington and was seldom there. By late summer 2025, his health was failing. The hormone deprivation drugs had stopped working, and his prostate cancer was metastasizing, leading to episodes of intense bone pain. He spent as much time as possible at the home in Lews he had shared with the President for so many years. He had a steady stream of visitors from church and enjoyed working as much as he could in the garden. The hospice nurses were superb at titrating the narcotics he needed keep the pain at bay but in a way that allowed him to stay as active as possible. Pastor Bob promised to stop by as soon as his travel schedule permitted. Baker Jimerson, who had recently separated from his wife, moved into the Pailer house to "support my dear friend."

In early 2026, when it was pretty clear the end was near, President Pailer came to Minnesota and spent the last week of Marco's life with him in their house. This created major traffic problems in Lews as numerous streets were either closed or rerouted. The skeet shooting club around the corner from the Pailer house also had to suspend operations for security reasons and because the shotgun discharges spooked the police dogs.

At the end, as Marco drifted in and out of consciousness, he said to the President, "Please find somebody who can satisfy you. I am so sorry I couldn't." He died with the next breath. Michelle cried softly and reflected alone for a few minutes about what might come next. Except for an hour here or there with Agent Jeffs, she had in many ways been alone her whole adult life.

The funeral for Marco Pailer was the biggest event in the history of Archangel Christian Church. It went off without a hitch, and Dr. Pailer's heroic efforts to cure young men with the Gender Confusion Syndrome were duly celebrated. At the request of Pastor Bob, the mainstream media was excluded from the services. There was no need for the good work of the National Center for Gender Confusion to take another beating on CNN and in the *New York Times*. The President looked incredible in her mourning dress and veil. *Vanity Fair* posted side-by-side comparative mourning outfit pictures of President Pailer and Tatiana Schrimpf from a few years earlier. The consensus from fashion commentators was that even though Michelle was more than 10 years older than Tatiana, she looked much better.

Both Pastor Bob and Judge Moon, who was in attendance, noticed time and time again that from beneath her veil, the President's eyes spent a lot of time locked on the Secret Service agent by the door. Due to commitments with U.S.A. Hockey at the Winter Olympics in Italy, the twins could not attend and released the following statement, "Dad fought a good fight and lost in overtime. Our task now is to stay focused on winning gold for Team U.S.A. here in Milan."

The Jones-Mulkey twins were also in Milan as Team 2-squared reunited for Team U.S.A. The gold medal game against Canada went down to the wire. With time running out, Bobby stole the puck and passed to Boris who was circling at center ice. Wayne found an angle on the Canadian defender and took the pass from Boris. He was in perfect position for the shot. However, Vlad had been streaking down the other side of the ice. Wayne dumped the puck to Vlad, who beat the goalie as the horn sounded. 2-1 U.S.A. for the gold.

43. The Second *Moon Report*

In the fall of 2025 as Marco's health was failing, there was nothing going on and the news cycle was essentially dead. The gridlock in Washington was perpetual, and with majorities in both houses and the reconfigured Supreme Court, the Democrats were biding their time until the 2026 midterms and the 2028 presidential election. In the absence of real or fake news, the commentariat started asking about when Judge Moon would finish his investigation into the death of President Schrimpf. Attorney General Trip Bush had similar questions, although he had heard through various grapevines that nothing would come of it.

Trip Bush met with Judge Moon in the spring of 2026, and Moon highlighted the key findings:

1) There was no evidence that rogue senior officers in the U.S. Navy had plotted to assassinate President Schrimpf.
2) The *USS Hilton* had in fact been 10 miles as opposed to five miles off the coast of Alabama.
3) The best available scientific evidence, and new classified computer simulations, made it "highly unlikely" that the microwave shotgun on the *Hilton* contributed in any meaningful way to the lightning strike that killed President Schrimpf.
4) High surface water temperature in close proximity to the 8th hole might have contributed to the lightning strike that killed President Schrimpf.
5) After being struck, President Schrimpf had received textbook medical care.

These results were released in a brief memo to the public along with several scientific documents to support conclusions 2-5. A confidential section of the report detailed a culture of "significant" drinking and womanizing by members of the Navy brass, most notably those who had been fighter pilots. It also detailed just how deeply Schrimpf was hated by the Navy as a result of his treatment of the late Senator Hannibal Hilton. Bush asked Moon if anything else interesting had popped up. Moon responded, "Not a thing."

The general public and mainstream media were supportive of what Moon had concluded. The *New York Times* called it a partial atonement for the "politically motivated hit job that Moon had performed on President McClintock with the first *Moon Report*."

Almost immediately, fringe elements of the remaining Schrimpf-istas and assorted conspiracy theorists generated a cottage industry of alternate facts and cover-up stories about what had really happened on that fateful day. Within a few weeks, regularly scheduled tour boats were available to take conspiracy enthusiasts "to the exact spot in the Gulf" where the *Hilton* fired the microwave shotgun.

A few days after meeting with Trip Bush, Judge Moon was invited to the White House for a photo opportunity and to officially present the findings of his report to President Pailer. Incredibly, he had never been in the Oval Office and had never seen the spot on the carpet where President McClintock had mounted "that woman." The semen stain on the Presidential Seal that was central to the work of the first Moon Investigation had been removed, but finally being at the scene of that infamous act was satisfying enough.

At the end of the photo op, Moon asked the President if he could visit with her privately for a few minutes. She readily agreed. Moon, who could still play the professor, simply said, "Madam President, can I give you a piece of friendly advice?" "Sure," Michelle replied. He said, "If I were you, I would turn the Cassandra off when you are exercising with Agent Jeffs," and then walked out of the Oval Office.

44.   A White House Wedding

Michelle hoped her secret was safe with Judge Moon, who based on the ability he had shown to look the other way during the "dormitory violations" scandal at Briles Baptist University, could keep his mouth shut.   However, Washington was a leaky town.   She shared her concerns with Agent Jeffs and proposed to him in the Oval Office.   She half-jokingly threatened to issue an executive order.

Jeffs loved a lot about President Pailer and was really attracted to her, but he was unsure about actually getting married to anyone, much less someone as politically rigid as Michelle Pailer.   He thought about it and thought about it.   When he considered what might happen if their secret got out, he kept coming back to "They can fire me, but they can't execute me."

A few weeks later, the twins visited her in the White House and Boris asked, "Mom, what's the deal with you and the secret agent dude?" Vladislav chimed in, "Is he really as buff as they say?"

Michelle asked the boys what they had heard and who they had heard it from.   They told her that Wayne and Bobby overheard their mom Tammy talking to their mom Helen about it and then relayed the information to them at an NHL promotional event.

Over the next few weeks, Agent Jeffs read everything he could about Michelle Pailer and came to believe that she was like an aspiring elite athlete who had gotten trapped in a doping culture and adopted a skewed perspective on "normal"—sort of a slow-motion brainwashing beginning when she was 14 or 15 years old.

He finally told the President that he "would consider marriage" if they dated publically for a while.   She was reluctant to do that and said, "What about the rumors, and the base?"

He responded, "They can fire you, but they can't execute you."

They started to be seen together in public, and Jeffs took a leave of absence from the Secret Service.   No one could believe it.   The twins connected immediately with Jeffs, who gave them input about optimizing their strength training and overall fitness.   He reminded them that in team sports like ice hockey "the legs feed the wolf" and suggested high-intensity interval training to take their fitness to the "next level." The conditioning program Jeffs outlined was far simpler, but much more intense than the twins had ever used before. He explained to the them, "that in order to be a maximalist, you must first be a minimalist." By being in even better shape, Boris and Vlad had their greatest seasons as pros.

Bruce and Kaye Jensen were thrilled that Michelle was finally involved with a regular guy and not some religious crackpot. They wondered if he might even be a Lutheran.

President Pailer and Andy Jeffs were married in the Rose Garden in the late summer of 2026.

As her personal satisfaction increased, her public persona softened, and people began to wonder if "Pailer was still a Pailerite."

The 2026 midterm elections resulted in no major changes in the balance of power in D.C.

45. Return to Rand

As President Jeffs (she took the last name Jeffs) gradually lost interest in her job and went on an extended honeymoon using Air Force One to fly her and First Gentleman Jeffs to exotic locations all over the world, Vice President Rand became the de facto president in all but name for the last 24 months of the Pailer/Jeffs term. He chaired Cabinet meetings, tried to work constructively with the Congress, negotiated various budget deals, met with foreign leaders, and behaved in a competent way. There were no major international crises, so issues related to chain of command were avoided.

The only minor incident occurred in when there was a civilian helicopter crash in Bora Bora during a state visit to French Polynesia. Several members of the paparazzi were badly injured when they were flying close to the beach in an effort to get photos of The President in a bikini or possibly less. Fortunately, First Gentleman Jeffs had been body surfing near the crash and used his superior swimming skills to personally rescue and tow several of the photographers to safety. He administered first aid on the beach.

Rand was actually able to pass some bipartisan legislation for the first time in years when he cobbled together an odd coalition of legislators from sugar states, freedom caucus members, and the few remaining Democrats who supported personal freedom. Working together, in a way that had not been seen in years, they passed a ban on sugar-sweetened beverage taxes at the state and local level. He hailed it as a "major victory for personal freedom."

The Internet search, marketing, and social media giant SIREN (maker of Cassandra) convinced Vice President Rand to champion a vast program of online voter registration and actual voting. SIREN argued that privacy concerns were overblown and any information they gleaned would "increase the efficiency of corporate marketing and thus spur economic growth." This was music to Rand's ears.

No one in either party was concerned about privacy anymore, and the Republicans bought into the idea when SIREN convinced them that with modern data mining, machine learning, and artificial intelligence techniques, there would be no more voter fraud. Their only condition was that any online voting-related effort be "fully privatized." SIREN convinced the Democrats that the SIREN plan was "a great way to increase turnout among their demographics."

SIREN had so much cash that they were able (as one Cook brother said to the other) "to mount a lobbying and influencing effort that makes what we have done over the years look like a bake sale." In addition to generous campaign contributions, every politician in the country who had a say on voting regulation got highly effective and customized pop-up ads whenever they used a computer. Elected officials from both parties also got private briefings explaining that the way the SIREN search engines worked, there would be a "small but real built-in natural edge" for incumbents.

The initiative passed easily, and Vice President Rand extolled it as another example of his efforts to work with both parties to "empower Americans and spur economic growth."

Slowly, the shadow that Schrimpf had cast over the Republican Party receded, and so-called normalcy returned.

Rand launched his ↦*Return to Rand as Fast as You Can*↦ campaign in mid-2027 and hammered on the economic themes he had been talking about since first being elected to the House of Representatives in the mid-1990s. His main competition was Texas Senator Thad Cross. However, Cross's wife Cheryl, a hedge fund manager, developed an unspecified debilitating illness, and Cross dropped out of the race to "take over the family business." The field was clear for Rand.

The only concern was that Rand typically answered all questions, about any topic, with a highly polished and almost automated variation of one of his favorite sounds bites. When he was asked what he wanted for his 56th birthday, Rand responded, "Lower taxes to stimulate economic growth." When asked what he wanted for Christmas, he responded, "An opportunity society dedicated to unshackling the creative potential of the American people." At Easter, he said he was hoping for "nothing less than the resurrection of the American Dream."
Those unusual responses aside, Rand swept the primaries and wrapped up the nomination early. Front organizations linked to the Cook brothers made sure he had essentially unlimited resources at his disposal for the general election campaign.

46. Sins of the Father

Mac Jackson was the answer to the Democrats' prayers. Jackson, who identified as African American, had been elected governor of Georgia in 2022 and was reelected by a wide margin in 2026. He was extremely articulate and had crossover appeal to white suburban voters. He also avoided the various traps that Bernard and de Rincon had fallen into during the 2020 and 2024 campaigns. Jackson was also big on economic growth and said repeatedly that the best social program was a good job. His triangulation approach to politics reminded analysts of the late Willie McClintock.

To stimulate growth in Georgia, he had worked closely with the Cook brothers' AESF to identify areas around Georgia that needed to be hardened against possible terrorist attacks including the threat of drone swarms. He partnered with the federal government to secure funding for a drone-proof dome over Sanford Stadium at the University of Georgia, and engineers at Georgia Tech were doing a pilot and feasibility study on the possibility of putting a huge dome over Augusta National Golf Course. The construction boom associated with these projects, and those in the works, generated a regional economic bonanza and enabled Jackson to increase public funding for education, housing, and health care.

Jackson's personal story was impressive. He was the son of a single mother in Nashville and became a basketball star at Vanderbilt University. Too small for the NBA, he obtained a law degree at Emory University and became a leading sports agent. He used his connections to develop a regional real estate and restaurant empire and cashed out at age 37 to pursue a life of public service.

His mother, Martha Jackson, made a good living as a session singer in Nashville while Mac was growing up. Her extended family was quick to note that their ancestors had been "house slaves" at the Hermitage Plantation near Nashville owned by President Andrew Jackson. Martha was an exotic-looking woman who was clearly mixed race, including at least some "Indian" as she put it. She had given up a promising solo career as a gospel singer to raise Mac. In the early 80s while she was barely 20, she had even made several appearances on the Grand Ole Opry singing gospel classics like *How Great Thou Art*. She appealed to anyone who liked gospel music. Her cover of *I Saw the Light* by Hank

Williams was the first single to simultaneously top the R&B, country, and gospel charts.

Only two people on earth knew who Mac's father was, Martha and the late Willie McClintock. McClintock was a big gospel fan. When he was governor of Tennessee, he saw her perform several times at the Opry when his wife Beth was out of town visiting her parents in the Chicago suburbs. He was so entranced after seeing Martha Jackson at the Opry one Saturday, he asked the state troopers in the governor's detail to see if she was willing to stop by the governor's mansion for a bite to eat after the show. She could hardly say no, and that was the story of the next few months—she could hardly say no.

Mac's "paper bag complexion" led Martha's family to assume she had gotten pregnant by a country music star, but she kept her mouth shut and McClintock found a spot for her on the state payroll. Ultimately she did well enough as a session singer to quit her state job and didn't need much if anything financially from McClintock. She hated the road and loved to sing, so she stayed at home raising Mac and doing session work.

Martha only soloed once again. In 2004, she sang *I Saw the Light* at the funeral of her friend, the legendary Ray Charles.

Mac Jackson always wondered who his father was, and some people said when he was older that he looked like a light-chocolate version of Willie McClintock. He wondered in the early 2000s why the ex-president—who had attended the University of Tennessee—was so interested in the Vanderbilt basketball program. As Jackson rose to prominence as a sports agent, McClintock frequently called when he was working the phones. "The Pres," as Mac called him, repeatedly urged him to get into "public life."

In 2021, when Jackson started to seriously think about running for governor, McClintock lined him up with some of the "real pros" he worked with over the years. During a face-to-face meeting in McClintock's Harlem office, they went over a map of Georgia, and McClintock detailed exactly what Jackson needed to do in each section of the state to run a successful race. He gave Jackson his old Georgia Rolodex to enhance his network of experienced political operatives all over the state. McClintock demonstrated the "McClintock Treatment" handshake and told Jackson "not to pay too much attention to the Analytics Assholes" like his wife had done in 2016 when she lost the election to Schrimpf. He finished by telling Jackson the fact he was single and interested in women was a plus and warned him to "stay away from white girls and dancers until *after* he won the election."

Over the next seven years, Jackson came to see this meeting as one of the most important meetings of his life. McClintock was 74 years old when they chatted face-to-face. He had an almost animal-like charisma that Jackson had seen in only a few of the very best athletes he had represented. The technical advice McClintock gave Jackson about running for governor was "spot on."

Jackson won in 2022 and again in 2026. Party leaders seeking to avoid the chaos of the 2020 and 2024 Democratic primaries reengineered the nominating rules and front-loaded the primary election calendar to favor a moderate like Jackson. The field was cleared rapidly, and Jackson appeared set.

The only odd thing was that the on-line Dredge Report started posting pieces with headlines like "Just How Black Is Mac Jackson?" Sometime in early 2027, a Republican operative grabbed a Harpoon Coffee cup Jackson had been drinking from at a meet-and-greet economic development event in Atlanta. A swab from the cup was sent to the MyDNA consumer genetic testing company. The results came back that Jackson's genetic makeup was 49% white, 48% black, and 3% Native American. Jackson blew the report off and said it was an opportunity to increase his outreach to Native American voters. Folks who knew his mother and had heard the rumor about the country music star and Martha Jackson figured that it was true. Out of curiosity, Martha Jackson got tested and her numbers came out 18% white, 76% black, and 6% Native American.

With the nominations of both parties set before Memorial Day, there was endless speculation about potential vice presidential picks but beyond that nothing much happened. Rand crossed the country touting the sugar tax bill as an example of his ability to work across the aisle and "bring America together." Jackson was always seen at one of the many vast construction sites he championed.

The Cook brothers were happy with either candidate, and while their sympathies were clearly with Rand, they were friendly with Jackson, who could actually get things done and was way ahead in the polls. His links to professional sports were also seen as a plus as Cook

Construction Conglomerated sought to make headway with the remaining NFL teams and bigger college programs that needed drone-proof domed stadiums.

Then political lightning struck. Dredge TV posted a documentary on Jackson, claiming that early in his career as a sports agent he had procured one or more large-breasted Asian strippers from the IWA Gold Club in Atlanta to service a "prominent NFL owner." The owners (there were actually several) lawyered up, and no one could ever prove anything. However, the Bernard/de Rincon wing of the Democratic Party leapt into action and demanded that Jackson suspend his campaign until a thorough and independent investigation could be completed. The investigation was inconclusive, in part because electronic records from the 2000s were primitive, closed-circuit cameras had not yet become ubiquitous, and any remaining electronic "bread crumbs" had been stored using formats that precluded their retrieval and analysis in 2028.

Only one of the women linked to the allegations could be located— "Jade Ming," who was employed as director of beverage cart services for the Schrimpf organization. She said nothing, hoping she might be able to sell her story to the tabloids down the road or that it might be bought as part of a "catch and kill" effort by one of the NFL owners she once knew.

Things got even weirder when Dredge reported they had DNA evidence confirming that Jackson was "closely related" to Willie McClintock. Several close relatives of McClintock had sent samples to one of the DNA ancestry sites that also worked on cold-case criminal investigations. It was straightforward for Dredge to get the DNA dots connected, and it turned out that it was clear a white Grand Ole Opry star was not the father of Mac Jackson.

Things seemed to settle down for the Jackson campaign and he was nominated as expected. By then, Jade Ming had negotiated a big deal to sell her story, and the drama started all over again. She had scrapbooks filled with revealing polaroid pictures of her, Jackson, and one or more NFL owners. Many included racy inscriptions and were autographed.

The Democratic National Committee called a late August emergency meeting. If Jackson was going to go, it had to be done quickly so his replacement could get on the ballot, and more importantly, the political bleeding could stop. Luckily for the Democrats, Vice President Rand was unable to leverage the chaos due to his laser-like focus on empowering Americans via lower taxes and the creation of economic opportunity for all. When asked about the "Ming matter," Rand said, "As your next president, I look forward to negotiating an expanded bilateral trade agreement with President Ming of the People's Republic that will increase economic freedom and opportunity in both the U.S. and China."

47. Return of the Beth

In New Mexico, as her program of personal growth and reconciliation progressed, Beth Campbell started again to pay attention to current events. She did this by listening to National Public Radio on an untraceable analog transistor radio that she used for no more than an hour per day while doing chores around the monastery or working in the garden. The low-dose peyote brought clarity to the absurdity of what she heard.

Beth began to wonder if her personal journey toward reconciliation might be a model to help change the dialogue in the country as a whole. She had to find out.

To find out, Beth borrowed her shaman's pickup truck and drove cross country to Washington, D.C. Along the way, she stayed in motels that accepted cash and left no trail. She had no cell phone and enjoyed the ride. She took her time and was careful to find a park for her daily martial arts practice. She traveled light with a map, one spare robe, a pair of huarache sandals, a walking stick, a change of underwear, and a toothbrush.

During the long drive, Beth frequently tuned the truck radio to classic country music stations and for the first time understood why her late husband Willie loved country music. As he frequently said, "If you played a country song backward you got sober, your mamma and dog were still alive, you were still married, your truck started, your kids loved you, and you still had a job." As she drove onward, Beth was hit by the feeling that America needed to play its collective country music song backward.

Beth pulled into suburban Chevy Chase early on Sunday, August 27th, and headed for her only daughter's house on Quincy Street. She was uncertain if Charlotte and her family would be home or spending the last weekend of the summer on Martha's Vineyard. She hoped— without attachment—that Charlotte would be in D.C. for the emergency meeting of the Democratic National Committee, of which she was a member.

Beth knocked on the door a few minutes before 6 a.m. Charlotte answered in her workout clothes. She had been getting ready to spend 30 minutes on the elliptical trainer before heading to the emergency

DNC meeting. Charlotte's husband and kids, as Beth guessed, were on Martha's Vineyard.

"Mom!" she cried as she grabbed her mother in tears.

"Where *the hell* have you been? I've missed you so much!"

"On a journey," Beth replied.

They went into the house, sat down, and talked. Beth gave Charlotte a rough outline of where she had been for the past almost six years. Charlotte brought her up to speed on her kids and a few other things. At 8 a.m. she told her mom that it was time for her to head downtown for the DNC meeting that was sure to dump Mac Jackson.

Beth asked if she could park on the street and spend the night. Beth said, "Of course" and hugged her mom. When she got out of the shower and headed out the door, her mother was gone, but the truck was parked on the street in front of the house.

Charlotte thought about what just happened. She was always tempted to be angry with her mother, but as she got older she realized being married to her father would have been a nine-ring circus. As battle hardened as her mom was, she was human and 40 or 50 years in a fishbowl was nothing she wanted for herself, her husband, and especially her kids.

Above all, Charlotte was mostly relieved that her mother was safe and thrilled to see her.

48. The Craig Walters Blockbuster

When Beth left her daughter's house, she walked about ½ mile to the Metro Station and took the Red Line into Washington. She got off at the stop closest to the Fox News studio. She walked to the studio knowing that, unless the Sunday morning TV lineup had changed, "Fox News Sunday" would be on with the hard-charging Craig Walters hosting.

She opened the door and saw the familiar face of Frank Russell, the large African American security guard who was always there, and said, "Hi, Frank."

Frank said, "Why, Mrs. McClintock! Where *the hell* have you been?"

"On a journey, Frank. I need to visit with Craig. Can you take me to him?"

Frank responded, "During the news break after he is done interviewing the VP."

As they chatted for a few minutes, Beth asked that if it wasn't too much to remember if he could use Campbell or better yet Beth from now on. Frank said, "No problem, Beth."

Craig Walters was in the middle of interviewing Vice President Rand. When he asked Rand about who he expected to replace Mac Jackson as his opponent on the top of the Democratic ticket, Rand responded, "Craig, I have heard all the names you have heard, but whoever it is, I am sure they will oppose my plan to cut taxes and unleash the entrepreneurial genius of the American people." Walters tried several other questions on the replace Mac Jackson topic and on variations on the theme.

When he pressed Rand on how low income taxes should go, Rand responded, "Look at how the country grew in the nineteenth century before there was *any* income tax. Craig, we went from 13 colonies on the East Coast to a world power in less than a hundred years without the income tax, didn't we? That's the type of long-term growth we project will occur when my plan is adopted."

Walters thanked Rand and said, "We'll be back after the news break with the former chair of the Democratic National Committee, Larry Stern, to get his take on the Jackson situation."

As Walters was chatting up Stern, Frank escorted Beth into the "Fox News Sunday" studio, looked at Walters, and said, "Craig, look what the cat dragged in."

Beth looked at Walters and simply said, "Craig, can we talk?"

Walters was speechless. Stern, who was getting older, felt his atrial fibrillation kick in.

Several of the production people and camera operators had worked in combat zones. They were unfazed and got Beth mic'd up, got Stern off the set, and brought Walters a shot of vodka (the breakfast of champions at Fox News).

The vodka did the trick and Walters regained his composure. When the news break ended, he said, "Ladies and gentlemen, a very special last-minute guest has been added to this morning's show—the former First Lady and 2016 Democratic presidential nominee, Beth Campbell. Ms. Campbell, welcome to the show."

Walters had a nearly photographic memory for news-related trivia and remembered how Beth had signed the note she left at her husband's funeral.

"It's truly a pleasure to see you again after all these years, Craig. Feel free to call me Beth." She said this with a tone far more sincere and authentic than any greeting he had ever received from any politician in his long career. It felt like his favorite aunt had just stopped by to see how he was doing.

"I am sure our viewers, and really everyone in the country, if not the world, is wondering what you have been up to for the past almost six years and what you are doing in Washington?" he asked.

"I am on a journey, Craig."

After a few more introductory questions including ones about her health, she replied, "Believe it or not, at nearly 80, I've never been in better shape. It is amazing what daily exercise, watching what you eat, and taking time for other people can do for your health."

Craig started to press her on the timing of her sudden reappearance. She responded with a series of what he later described as "political koans," and Craig then went to the heart of the matter. "Look, Ms. Campbell—Beth—a lot of people in my business, in politics, and all over the country are going to see what is happening today—this incredible interview—as some sort of calculated Beth in Zen master's clothing effort by you to make the greatest political comeback since Richard Nixon. How do you answer that?"

Beth replied calmly, "First Craig, over the past nearly six years if there is one thing I have learned, it is to learn how to ignore."

"Second, Richard Nixon had many good domestic policy ideas that got lost in the chaos of Vietnam, Watergate, and his own demons. We can all learn a lot by studying his life. A few of the problems confronting him were beyond his control, but like most of us, he created many, if not most, of his own."

She finished by saying, "If my memory serves me right, I believe the late Senator Kennedy said, more than once, that his biggest legislative regret was not supporting Nixon's health care plan." Walters responded, "Ms. Campbell—Beth—your memory does serve you right, and that will not be surprising to anyone who has known you as long as I have."

By that time, the emergency DNC meeting had been suspended so the attendees could watch the spectacle unfolding on Fox News (a network that most of them had never watched). A big crowd gathered outside the Fox studios.

The interview lasted about 45 minutes and included almost no specific answers about anything. Beth's only comments about policy were the reference to Ted Kennedy and the Nixon health care plan. Walters noted the lack of specifics and said, "Look Beth, six years ago, and certainly in 2016, you would have had detailed policy responses to almost every question I've asked this morning. What gives?"

She replied calmly, "Craig, over the past nearly six years, I've learned that no one cares how much you know until they know how much you care."

As a result of the thousands of interviews he had done, Walters had a keen sense of when to wrap it up. He closed by asking, "Before we end, can you tell us anything about your plans going forward?" Beth responded that she intended to take the Metro back to her daughter's house, get off a few stops early so she could walk a couple of miles, and make some lunch. She also said she had some laundry to do, hoped to take a nap, and then catch up with her daughter over a home-cooked meal when "Charlotte returns from the DNC meeting." Beyond that, she said, "I have to start driving back to New Mexico in a few days and return the truck I borrowed to get here." The owner, she said, "needs it to haul the firewood he is chopping for the winter before it starts to snow."

Finally, Walters said, "If I can ask just one more question, why Fox News? An organization that could hardly be called friendly to you or your late husband."

"Craig," she said with a tear in her eye, "Over the years I have said many negative things about Fox viewers, including labeling some as unredeemable. I want to apologize to those people because, if I have learned anything over the past few years, it is that no one is unredeemable."

When they broke for the next news break, Walters thanked Beth for stopping by and turned to his producer and said, "Whatever becomes of this, it will be the most watched thing I have ever done." Beth overheard this, turned to Craig, smiled and said, "Craig, don't look at the scoreboard." She then left the building via a side entrance to avoid the crowds that had formed on the street and proceeded back to Chevy Chase as planned. The code on Charlotte's garage was still 2016, and she let herself into the house and let the rest of her day unfold.

In the 45 minutes she had been on the air, Fox News and the other networks rounded up the usual suspects from the commentariat. They spent the rest of the day breaking down "what the sudden reappearance of Beth Campbell McClintock might mean for the Jackson situation, the Democratic Party, and the 2028 general election."

When Charlotte returned home, exhausted from the meeting, Beth made her an omelet and poured her a glass of wine. Beth had unplugged the cable box to avoid the temptation to turn the TV on. They spent the rest of the evening catching up on the grandchildren. Charlotte asked if she was really planning to drive back to New Mexico. "First thing in the morning," was Beth's response. Charlotte thought for a minute and asked, "Can I come along?"

"Of course you can."

Charlotte called her husband and kids and told them the plan. Her mom was in bed by 9 p.m. to make sure she was rested for the drive.

The headline in the *New York Post* was:
"SHE'S BACK!"

49. The Drive

After a light breakfast, Beth and Charlotte left early Monday morning to beat traffic. Beth convinced Charlotte to travel light, so there was no real packing that needed to be done. They were off before 6 a.m. with almost nothing in the truck except a couple of high-end travel mugs full of Harpoon Dark Roast.

Other than saying good morning, Beth did not stop to chat with the TV reporters who had staked out the house, so they followed her out of town. A couple of vintage Priuses with faded "I'm with Beth" bumper stickers also joined the caravan. Beth agreed it was O.K. for Charlotte to use her iPhone 21 to help with navigation, and they headed south into Virginia. They talked the morning away while listening to classic country music stations.

At 11 a.m., they got off the highway and pulled into a small town with a nice park. Beth walked briskly around the park for 30 minutes and did some calisthenics-like exercises and martial arts movements with her walking stick. Charlotte did the same. This was all broadcast live, and several of the Prius drivers and passengers joined them.

Beth then suggested they get some lunch. Charlotte responded that the only thing available was fast food. "Then McDonald's it is!" said Beth. They ordered two cheeseburgers, a small bag of fries to split, and two kid-sized drinks with sugar.

On the way out of the McDonald's, a reporter yelled, "Are you trying to send a message to the liberal elites about their war on fast food?" Beth thought for a minute and said, "When I was a little girl, one of my favorite things to do with my dad was go for a burger at McDonald's. You got a small burger, a tiny bag of fries, and maybe eight ounces of Coke. No one died, and we were all skinny back then." For the next 24 hours, the policy implications of this simple piece of personal history were parsed on all the cable news channels.

Brief ad hoc and headline-generating "Beth Briefings," as they became known, occurred at every stop they made. When asked about a group of bikers that had joined the caravan, she replied, "They are some great guys, and I only hope they will be wearing helmets." This led to more questions on safety and health topics, and Beth spoke in favor of not smoking, vaccinations, daily exercise, seat belts, and dietary moderation.

On guns, she noted that most potentially dangerous activities, like operating heavy equipment or even driving a car, require extensive training, testing, and "recertification at regular intervals." "You can't," she said, "just buy a plane and start flying it."

When the ongoing drug crisis came up one day, after saying "life can be very painful," she spoke at length about the need for layers of compassion and various ways that people could learn to deal with "existential pain and learned helplessness," which she felt were "at the root of the problem." She quoted the psychiatrist and Holocaust survivor Viktor Frankl and said, "When we are no longer able to change a situation, we are challenged to change ourselves."

When a reporter shouted, "What about the Russians?" in a rare question about foreign policy, Beth responded, "I really enjoy Chekhov." The questions then turned to fiction, and she commented on how short stories are great "if you don't have time to commit to a novel." She went on to recommend stories by John Cheever and Raymond Carver. She said "Cathedral" by Carver was especially good.

One day the caravan was passed by a couple of ambulances, and she was asked about health care. She responded, "I am no longer up on the details, but unless something has changed, there are pretty good plans that cover everyone and provide plenty of choice in places like the Netherlands and Singapore. Maybe we could learn something from them." She also commented on the excellent plan federal employees and Congress enjoyed and said perhaps we should "give the people what Congress has."

The headline in the next day's *Washington Post* read:
"Beth Says Give People What Congress Has"

All of this kept the media and commentariat working at a frenzied pace, and as one analyst pointed out, "no one has gotten this much free media since Richard Schrimpf did in 2016."

Not even close.

As the caravan took a circuitous path back to New Mexico, Craig Walters, who occasionally joined the media pool covering the caravan, asked when they might finally arrive at their destination. She said, "Craig, as you well know, it is all about the journey and not the destination." As stale as that comment was, the media even nodded their heads in approval. There were no follow-up questions.

The headline in the next day's *New York Times* read:
"Beth Says Country on Journey"

The journey statement led to several positive columns in *The Times* by the noted columnist Brooks Davidson about the "New Beth" and about the "wisdom and common sense embedded in what she is saying."

Polling data started showing her winning a race against Rand, but she was not a candidate and despite meeting 8-12 hours every day for weeks, the various factions of the Democratic Party could not settle on a replacement for Jackson. The polling numbers for Beth did, however, evoke concern by the Secret Service. The head of the Secret Service made some quiet inquiries through Charlotte and was told, "My mom doesn't think it is necessary." The press also started asking questions about Secret Service protection, and Beth responded, "I will be 80 years old soon and am no longer worried too much about anything."

One day, she came out of one of the last remaining bookstores in the country with a copy of *Pray to the Deity of Your Choice* by Dr. Bob Emily. When questioned about her love of reading, she responded, "There is nothing like the feel of a book in your hands and nothing better than reading to your children."

Several times large crowds formed spontaneously in parking lots and she spoke briefly from the back of the truck. At nearly 80, her voice could still carry, but the "I know best" tone was gone as she encouraged people to "not mistake activity for achievement." She reminded young people in the crowd to "Control yourself so others won't have to." She closed these impromptu speeches with the simple reminder, "Don't let what you can't do interfere with what you can do."

These sayings and some of her other utterances began to appear on bumper stickers across the country that sold like hotcakes via the SIREN e-commerce site. This time they were seen on all sorts of cars and trucks. Way more than what the late President Schrimpf used to refer to as the "Prius Crowd." The most popular one was:

How Much Do You Care?

When Beth got to Chicago, she went to Wrigley Field to see her beloved Cubs play a late-season game against the St. Louis Cardinals. The Cubs were experiencing a team-wide batting slump, and their grip on first place was slipping. When asked if she had any advice for the struggling Cubs, she simply reminded them to "get a pitch to hit."

When the dean of conservative commentators, and big-time baseball fan, William George (he was also the only prominent truly conservative writer in the country who never had even a mild case of Schrimpf fever) saw this on ESPN's "Baseball Tonight," the light went on. He knew that "get a pitch to hit" was the mantra of the great Ted Williams, the last player to bat 400. He connected the dots and wrote, "Over the past month, Beth Campbell has found more than one pitch to hit, and she is knocking them out of the park."

Toward the end of the caravan, they passed the huge sinkhole just outside Rapture City, Oklahoma. The sinkhole had occurred during the fracking boom of the 2010s and was seen as a cautionary tale about the environment. When the environment came up during the next Beth Brief, she said she favored "conservation, renewables, and nukes." The nukes comment caught the media completely off guard, and for a few minutes the sort of aggressive questioning that was typical of 2016 made a comeback. Beth said she had learned a lot from some friends who live in Los Alamos. She urged the media, "Look at how many people die each year from air pollution."

Beth and Charlotte had reached the monastery on October 1st. Charlotte left the next day after more than a month of connecting with her mother in a way she never had before. As a parting gift, Beth gave Charlotte an old laptop and told her she had been using it to send the occasional email via encrypted NeutronMail. She also told her an IT guy from Los Alamos, who spent time at the monastery, had provided her with the laptop, which was loaded with Particle software.

"A really neat feature of the laptop," she said to Charlotte, "is untraceable Neutrino browser."

The TV trucks and RVs that now made up the caravan were parked outside the gate. The Cubs went on a collective hitting terror, their pitching held, and they won the 2028 World Series. Beth listened to the games on the radio.

50. Revenge of the Analytics Assholes

The Analytics Assholes (AAs), as the late President Willie McClintock called them, all landed on their feet after the debacle of 2016. Several of them ended up at SIREN, where they used their technical skills and political connections to drive the online voting initiative that Vice President Rand was so excited about.

In early September, the network of tech players (AAs) from the Beth 2016 campaign regrouped virtually and started figuring out how to use the "electronic environment" to draft Beth and propel her to victory in nine short weeks. Besides knowing the ins and outs of the online voter system SIREN was running in most jurisdictions, enough of them had gained leadership positions at SIREN to purge any conservative programmers and engineers from the organization.

It was, as one of them later said, like "shooting fish in a barrel." They worked feverishly and in a matter of days laid the groundwork for Beth to be on the ballot in all but a few states. They used data mining, machine learning, and artificial intelligence (AI) to automate their outreach efforts. This allowed the AAs to identify likely Beth voters and likely Rand voters and then "sculpt" opinion as needed. The bumper stickers were just one example.

Beth returned to her routine at the monastery. When she left the monastery and went for a hike or visited Santa Fe, the media kept the questions coming, and she responded with brief and mostly banal (although obviously useful) answers. When asked if she was willing to debate VP Rand, she said, "I'm not into arguing anymore but am willing to have a friendly discussion with my friend the Vice President."

The friendly discussion was scheduled for late October with Craig Walters serving as the moderator. The decisive exchange occurred when the topic of "racial dog whistles" came up. Beth responded that she had always admired the approach on race that Rand's political mentor the late Kemp Jackson, a long-serving congressman and former NFL quarterback from Buffalo, had taken. Rand responded by saying he was more worried about real vs. imaginary dog whistles and that "real dog whistles are no longer manufactured anywhere in the U.S., and as part of my economic empowerment, job creation, and tax cutting plan, I will bring the manufacture of real dog whistles back to the United States."

"Dog trainers across the country," he went on, "deserve nothing less than whistles stamped *made in USA*."

Within hours, the AAs had incorporated this exchange into the sculpting algorithms, and within 48 hours, Rand's numbers were in the toilet.

51. The Bethslide

For the first election since 2016, there was no drama on election day. Beth won states with more than 450 electoral votes and got just less than 60% of the popular vote. SIREN Election Central had tabulated, checked, and *validated* the results by midnight West Coast time. Turnout had never been higher. No evidence of voter fraud or election hacking by hostile foreign powers was found.

In the next few days, the commentariat developed three main explanations for the results:
1) The "Campbell message."
2) The inability of Vice President Rand "to pivot and discuss issues beyond tax cuts."
3) The fact that the Democrats had clearly won "the high-stakes bet on outsourcing the election to SIREN."

President-elect Beth had been following the election on the radio. At sunrise the next morning, she went to the gate of the monastery and simply thanked the voters. When asked about her next steps, Beth said, "I plan to not let the urgent crowd and the important and hope to drive to Washington when the firewood is delivered sometime after Thanksgiving." In the meantime, she would ask her daughter (who knew everyone in politics) to help with the transition.

She then headed to a secluded hut in the Sangre de Cristo Mountains for several days of intense reflection. She met the medicine man there, and with the help of a bit of low-dose peyote, her legislative priorities for the first 100 days emerged and became clear in her mind.

52. Binders of Qualified Candidates

When Charlotte returned home, she conferred with her husband Smith Erikson. Smith had been the designated "adult in the room" as CEO of SIREN when it grew explosively in the late 2000s and 2010s. He retired a rich man and spent his time serving on corporate boards, evaluating and advising start-ups, and generally being a "wise man" on all things tech. He and Charlotte discussed how best to identify and vet potential Cabinet appointees and other high government officials that required confirmation by the Senate.

Erikson said there was a straightforward solution to solve the challenge in the most efficient and "idiot proof" way possible. He then outlined how the Geometry start-up he had been working with could easily identify and generate "binders of qualified candidates."

"How's that?" Charlotte asked.

"It can easily be accomplished by an algorithm," he said. He then told her that Geometry could use data mining, machine learning, and AI to literally search the entire population for qualified candidates. He explained how McKinney Consulting routinely used Geometry's proprietary algorithms in personnel searches for large corporations. Geometry also sold a line of decision support tools for criminal sentencing and parole deliberations.

"What are the next steps?" Charlotte asked.

First, Smith said, they needed to come up with a list of minimal qualifications for each office including screening for any obvious "disqualifiers." Second, they would then determine the ideological and philosophical alignment characteristics each potential candidate had with her mother. A list of key elements in "these domains" could be generated by searching everything Beth had written or said that was in an electronic database starting with her honors thesis from college or even the valedictorian address she gave at her high school graduation in 1966.

As a secondary screen, he explained, they could include searches of her dad and other political figures Beth admired. Some facets of Nixon's unrealized domestic agenda came to mind. They could then add more recent polling data to get a better idea about what "might stick."

Demographic filters could be applied to the screening results, ensuring the list of potential nominees that "looked like America." The final step would be to match the three to five candidates who made the final cut for alignment with pressure points and other characteristics and preferences of opinion leaders in the media and, most importantly, members of the Senate.

"Smith," Charlotte asked, "how long will all of this take and who will pay for it?"

"A couple of weeks, tops," he answered. "Almost all of the data is readily available, and a lot of this can be done with Geometry's generic platforms. Any hand curation will come at the very end when your mom has to interview folks and pick a final candidate. For the lower-level positions, the algorithms should be able to handle the entire process and provide a single name. Plus, you and I can easily cover the cost and by spending a couple of million dollars. This will likely increase the value of Geometry severalfold and prime it for the IPO market."

He closed his Geometry sales pitch to his wife by saying, "There is no better way to do this quickly and efficiently and de-risk the whole process. The Geometry approach will allow us to cast the widest possible net and check all the important boxes."

Charlotte asked two additional questions. She wanted to know what would happen if one of the finalists said no and how big a stake she and Smith had in Geometry. Smith answered, "We can build the likelihood of saying yes into the screening. If someone unexpectedly says no, a couple of candidates with basically identical characteristics will be waiting in the wings." He then added, "We have a 17% stake in the company."

"Let's do it," she said.

Because Beth had no running mate, the only possible drama remaining before the inauguration was who would be the vice president. This would be decided by the Electoral College, which was scheduled to meet in early December. Smith said they could use Geometry to "pilot the binders project" and come up with some names.

The vice presidential pilot project came up with several names including Fred Westwood, who was a former NBA player and one of the greatest 3-point shooters in league history. Westwood was also a Hall of Fame coach. He was known to be extremely well organized, flexible, an excellent speaker, and completely conversant on public policy. His only potential black mark was that he could have an extremely foul mouth in private.

Charlotte thought it was an inspired "out-of-the-box" pick. When she conveyed the recommendation to her mom, Beth (a big sports fan) was thrilled. Westwood was contacted by Smith Erikson and he readily agreed to the idea. A call was arranged with the President-elect, and Westwood promised to watch his language and suggested the President-elect might enjoy reading the *Inner Game of Tennis*. Beth thanked him for the recommendation and said she had read it a couple of years ago. She then asked him to work on the cussing and closed by reminding him to "control yourself so others don't have to."

Westwood was easily approved by the Electoral College and became the Vice President–elect.

Geometry did a great job with the rest of the searches, and the only tweak they added to the process Smith Erikson had outlined to Charlotte was building a five-point "tech friendliness" scale into the selection algorithms: 1 = tech hostile, 2 = mostly tech hostile, 3 = tech neutral, 4 = mostly tech positive, and 5 = tech enthusiast. They built enough randomness into the process to make sure that while no 1s emerged as finalists, almost no 2s, a few 3s, with mostly 4s and few 5s did emerge. The key, they knew, was to not overdo it and sculpt opinion.

53. Inauguration Day

The run-up to the inauguration was perhaps the smoothest ever. Beth arrived, by truck, in D.C. in early December. She had taken a southern route to avoid any weather and to maximize her ability to get classic country radio stations in the truck during the drive.

She moved into the spare room of Charlotte and Smith's house in Chevy Chase. The grandkids and their friends loved it, especially the mock sword play that Grandma Beth performed with her walking stick as part of the martial arts drills she did on a daily basis in the backyard.

The transition team, led by Charlotte, was lauded as hyper efficient, and each Cabinet candidate that was announced was seen as at least a solid, if not excellent or even inspired, choice. No skeletons were found in any closets. The only thing remotely scandalous was that a clip of Westwood was run showing him dropping "multiple F-bombs" while excoriating referees during an NBA playoff game. The clip was almost 10 years old, and the incident came after a really bad call on his fiery defensive star Raymond Brown during a playoff game. When asked about the clip, Westwood simply said that his language was "something I clearly need to work on." The now retired Brown, who had a regular gig on ESPN's "SportsCenter," came to the defense of his old coach saying, "The refs deserved it." He added that "the guys are really looking forward to finally visiting the White House."

During planning for the inauguration, Beth politely declined any help with her speech and told the event coordinators that she would not be using any Teleprompters during what would be a very short speech. When she met the director of the Marine Corps Band, she asked if Duke the trumpet player from Hawaii she had heard several times while serving as Secretary of Defense was still in the band. To her delight, the director replied he was indeed. She pulled a large conch shell out from under her robe and asked him to give it to Duke and to instruct Duke to sound the conch when the time was right.

Because there was no chief justice, it was unclear which justice should administer the oath of office. The seven remaining justices drew straws, and the honors fell to 93-year-old Justice Ruth Bader Ginsburg. She was fine with the President-elect using the *Tibetan Book of the Dead* in lieu of a standard Bible for the swearing in.

The weather was good on Inauguration Day, not too hot, not too cold. The dignitaries on the temporary stage on the west side of the Capital were all there. President Pailer/Jeffs, at age 60, remained statuesque and beautiful beyond belief. As always, the dress she wore accentuated her impressive bustline and trim waist. Her only rival in the looks department was the First Gentleman, who was extremely handsome and the only man on the stage wearing an athletic cut suit, unusual for someone 54 years old. Both the President and First Gentleman were extremely tan from spending a lot of time on tropical islands during the many state visits and fact-finding missions they had been doing over the past 24 months.

After the swearing-in, rumors circulated around town that several female Fox News reporters and anchors had complained when data showed Michelle got more screen time than they did in aggregate.

When it came time for the oath of office, Beth Campbell pulled the hood of her cloak back, removed her Ray Bans, and walked to the podium. Backed by her daughter and grandchildren, she placed her hand on the *Tibetan Book of the Dead* and was sworn in.

She moved to the microphone and addressed the massive crowd out on the National Mall.

"Thank you, thank you, thank you very much," she said and then began,

"My friends, the past few months have been very unusual. The temptation is to give a long and hopefully inspirational speech. That would be the easy thing to do. Instead, today I want to sing a song for you that has become very meaningful for me over the past six years and especially as I traveled the country the past few months."

"The song," she said, "is by Hank Williams, and if you know the words please join in and sing along."

She then cleared her throat and started to sing.

I wandered so aimless, life filled with sin
I wouldn't let my dear Savior in
Then Jesus came like a stranger in the night
Praise the Lord, I saw the light

I saw the light, I saw the light
No more darkness, no more night
Now I'm so happy, no sorrow in sight
Praise the Lord, I saw the light

Just like the blind man, I wandered along
Worries and fears, I claimed for my own
Then like the blind man, that God gave back his sight
Praise the Lord, I saw the light

I saw the light, I saw the light
No more darkness, no more night
Now I'm so happy, no sorrow in sight
Praise the Lord, I saw the light

When Beth Campbell finished singing, Sgt. Major Duke Aikau, USMC, sounded the conch. The unamplified blast reverberated down the Mall and reportedly shook the columns at the Lincoln Memorial. Sgt. Major Aikau later said the force of the sound came "straight from Pele."

President Campbell pulled up her hood, put her Ray Bans on, grabbed the hands of her grandchildren, walked off the stage, and headed toward the White House. No one in the media or political establishments had any idea about what to do next. Except, that is, for Michelle Jeffs. Her eyes had been locked on her Andy since they had mounted the temporary stage on the Capital 45 minutes earlier. He had truly never looked better.

54. Epilogue

In 2040, both sets of twins (Boris, Vlad, Wayne, and Bobby) were inducted into the Hockey Hall of Fame. They asked to be introduced "as a unit." The three mommies sat side by side with no hint of tension. During her post presidency, Michelle returned to Redeemer Lutheran and became a leading advocate of an inclusive take on the Bible. Andy Jeffs, who had been setting age group world records in a number of track and field events, looked as fit as ever at 208 pounds.

When it came time for the twins to be introduced, 100-year-old Bruce Jensen, upright and still vigorous with a closely cropped gray buzz cut, walked out onto the stage wearing the University of Minnesota blazer he had been awarded in the late 1950s. His comments were brief, and he said, "The success of all four boys shows that when you work with kids the keys are to focus on the person first, the athlete second, and the player third and then let good things happen." He continued and said the sustained excellence and focus all four had shown over the years demonstrated what happens when you "don't confuse activity with achievement."

About the author: Michael J. (Mike) Joyner is a medical doctor and researcher who lives in Rochester, Minnesota. He was once a pretty good distance runner and has written many scientific articles. This is his first novel. His Twitter handle is @DrMJoyner.

Cover art by Bruce Doscher https://brucedoscher.com/

Acknowledgments: I would like to thank members of my family and many friends who listened to me yap about the contents of *Michelle the Archangel* as it took shape. I would also like to thank several anonymous proofreaders who prefer to remain anonymous so their kids and family members don't find out they have read this book.

36929096R00078

Made in the USA
San Bernardino, CA
25 May 2019